Flooded Floors to Open Doors: A Sanctuary Reclaimed

OrangeBooks Publication

1st Floor, Rajhans Arcade, Mall Road, Kohka, Bhilai, Chhattisgarh 490020
Website: **www.orangebooks.in**

© Copyright, 2024, Author

All rights reserved. No part of this book may be reproduced, stored in a retrieval system, or transmitted, in any form by any means, electronic, mechanical, magnetic, optical, chemical, manual, photocopying, recording or otherwise, without the prior written consent of its writer.

First Edition, 2024

ISBN: 978-93-6554-591-3

FLOODED FLOORS
—— TO ——
OPEN DOORS

A SANCTUARY RECLAIMED

VIVEK BUDAKOTI

OrangeBooks Publication
www.orangebooks.in

Preface

Disasters have a way of intrusion and creating chaotic puddles into human existence. They strip away the superfluous, leaving behind only what truly matters i.e. resilience, courage, and the will to persevere. This story is not merely an account of survival during a catastrophic flood; it is a testament to the indomitable human spirit, the power of leadership, and the bonds that strengthen in the face of adversity.

In a world where luxury hotels symbolize opulence and indulgence, rarely does one consider the sheer effort it takes to keep their sanctity intact during turbulent times. As a General Manager of a bustling hotel, I was tasked with an extraordinary challenge when relentless rains and rising waters threatened to submerge not only the physical structure but also the morale of everyone within it.

This book is not just my story; it is the story of my team, the silent warriors who refused to let the flood dictate our fate. It is about the patrons who found a home in our hotel amidst chaos, and the community that stood resilient in the face of destruction. It is about balancing professional duties with personal concerns, about leading with resolve while quieting the storm of emotions within.

Every chapter is woven from the threads of reality moments of fear, triumph, exhaustion, and hope. It recounts the journey of transforming despair into determination, rubble into renewal, and challenges into opportunities. From navigating submerged basements and debris-filled corridors to celebrating moments of collective prayer and restoration, the narrative encapsulates a rollercoaster of emotions and experiences.

This book is a tribute—to the team that stood by me unwaveringly, to my family who remained my silent strength, and to the countless unsung heroes who rose to the occasion. It is a reminder that even in the face of nature's fury, humanity finds a way to rebuild, to persevere, and to hope.

Through these pages, I hope to inspire anyone who faces their own storms, literal or metaphorical, to stand tall, face the odds, and rebuild every aspect brick by brick, step by step.

Welcome to the story of a flood, a hotel, and the people who refused to let it drown. Welcome to *"The Sanctuary Reclaimed."*

Acknowledgments

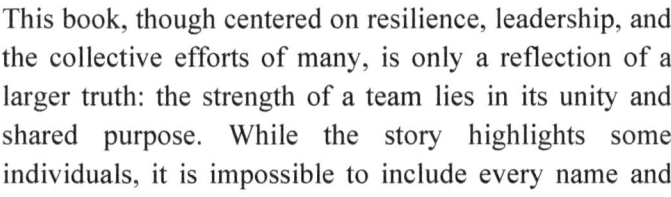

This book, though centered on resilience, leadership, and the collective efforts of many, is only a reflection of a larger truth: the strength of a team lies in its unity and shared purpose. While the story highlights some individuals, it is impossible to include every name and every contribution, but each effort was indispensable and deeply valued.

A special mention goes to the interns from **SRIHM Institute Kolkata**, whose integrity, dedication, and resilience were a hallmark of their character. My heartfelt gratitude extends to the entire faculty of SRIHM, whose nurturing and ethos were clearly evident in the students' actions during the crisis. To the parents and families of these young professionals, thank you for instilling values that shone brightly in the darkest hours.

To the **Housekeeping Team**, your tireless efforts from start to finish—and even long after— are the unsung backbone of our recovery. The **Kitchen Stewarding** who kept the area hygienic and clean despite of shortage of water and **Food & Beverage Service Teams**, who served everyone with unwavering smiles, and the **Kitchen Team**, who went above and beyond their core duties, taking on heavy tasks with grace and determination, you are heroes in every sense.

The **Front Office Team**, always at the guests' disposal, and the **Engineering Team**, who met every challenge at lightning speed, thank you for your commitment and ingenuity. **Finance team**, thank you for your extraordinary efforts in coordination and procurement of various things which were absolutely necessary for the recovery of the hotel. To the **Sales Manager**, **Human Resources Manager**, **drivers**, and everyone else who supported the recovery efforts, whether physically or virtually, your contributions were invaluable.

I am deeply grateful for the faith placed in me by the **Promoters and my Organization**, whose trust and confidence were a source of immense motivation. That faith not only strengthened my resolve but also enabled me to inspire others around me.

Finally, to the **Guests** who stood by us during the most trying times, your patience, empathy, and unwavering support were nothing short of extraordinary. You reminded us that in moments of crisis, we are all branches of the same tree, connected and interdependent.

To anyone I may have inadvertently missed in these acknowledgments or the forthcoming chapters, please accept my sincerest apologies. Your efforts are no less significant and remain deeply appreciated.

As a final note, the names of characters in this book have been changed or represented by their designations to protect their privacy and for other necessary reasons.

Thank you all for being a part of this journey.

Contents

Chapter - 1
The Unsettling Calm Before the Storm 1

Chapter - 2
The Art of War Against Nature's Fury 4

Chapter - 3
Drawing Battle Lines 7

Chapter - 4
The Call to Action 10

Chapter - 5
A Long Night of Vigilance and Uncertainty 16

Chapter - 6
Awakening the Warrior Within 21

Chapter - 7
Navigating the Storm's Chaos 26

Chapter - 8
The Deceptive Calm 31

Chapter - 9
Battling Time and the Unseen Surge 36

Chapter - 10
The Unsettling Harbinger 43

Chapter - 11
Holding the Fort Amidst the Rising Tide 48

Chapter - 12
  The First Breach 54

Chapter - 13
  Nature's Ballet: When the City Dances with
  the Moon.. 59

Chapter - 14
  Armoured for the Battle... 63

Chapter - 15
  Fortifying the Stronghold 69

Chapter - 16
  A War of Flow and Force 75

Chapter - 17
  An Unnatural Pattern 80

Chapter - 18
  The Deluge Unleashed... 83

Chapter - 19
  The Missing Piece 87

Chapter - 20
  The Rising Tide 91

Chapter - 21
  Rising Challenges, Deepening Waters 96

Chapter - 22
  Shutting Down the Heartbeat 100

Chapter - 23
  The Weight of the Sky... 104

Chapter - 24
  The Art of Survival.. 108

Chapter - 25
  Candlelight and Crisis 112

Chapter - 26
  Cooling the Heat of Crisis 116

Chapter - 27
  The Weight of Darkness 120

Chapter - 28
  The Morning Without Respite 124

Chapter - 29
  Tapping the Skies 129

Chapter - 30
  Power in Crisis 133

Chapter - 31
  A Boat, a Promise, and a War Cry 139

Chapter - 32
  The Weight of Trust 146

Chapter - 33
  The Weight of Water 151

Chapter - 34
  The Siege of Survival 157

Chapter - 35
  Dawn of Relief 163

Chapter - 36
  The Aftermath of the Deluge 167

Chapter - 37
  The Race to Recovery 171

Chapter - 38
 The Price of Progress 176

Chapter - 39
 Restoring Heights 180

Chapter - 40
 The Symphony of Revival 184

Chapter - 41
 Faith,Family,andFarewell
 (The Missing Chapter) 189

Chapter - 0
 Lessons from the Storm - A Guide to Resilience ... 194

Chapter — 1

The Unsettling Calm Before the Storm

Flooded Floors to Open Doors: A Sanctuary Reclaimed

The monsoon rains had settled in like an uninvited guest, and the city of Vadodara was already soaked to its brim by Sunday morning. But today on Monday, the downpour felt different— relentless and menacing. As I lounged at home for an extended day off to mark the auspicious occasion of Krishna Janmashtami, a sense of déjà vu tugged at me. It was a day meant for festivity and reflection, but my mind could not shake off the worry brought by the rhythmic drum of rain against the windowpanes.

Why? Because I knew this pattern all too well. *Janmashtami* had become synonymous with torrential rain for as long as I could remember. The skies poured harder every year, as if honoring the occasion in their own way. And today was no different.

Despite being physically away from the hotel, I found myself immersed in work, and every fifteen minutes my phone buzzed with updates from the housekeeping and engineering teams, each message forcing me to glance at the status of the hotel and the rising water levels of the *Vishwamitri River*. It was an old, unpredictable acquaintance; this river, which flowed just a few hundred meters behind the hotel—close enough to be a concern and far enough to pretend otherwise.

As hours passed, my concern grew deeper. "What's the current status?" I typed it out, firing off yet another message to the team. The replies were swift but worrisome: *Water levels of the river are rising, sir. Engineering is keeping an eye on the basement. Housekeeping is clearing any potential hazards.*

The pattern continued—every update punctuating the steady fall of rain. My instincts were on high alert, but I kept telling myself it would be fine. After all, we had weathered such storms before. But somewhere, deep down, I knew we were only one step away from the calm turning into chaos.

And Janmashtami wasn't over yet.

Chapter - 2

The Art of War Against Nature's Fury

There is a saying: *In the face of adversity, do not rely on opinion—rely on facts.* As a General Manager, I have learned to keep a calm head during crises. But my days spent in a military hostel had honed something deeper within me: the ability to assess threats like a strategist preparing for battle.

With the hotel's future, and the safety of our guests at stake, I decided it was time to switch from passive monitoring to active data collection. Sitting on my living room couch, laptop and phone sprawled around me, I have dived into a rigorous process of information- gathering.

Local Weather Forecast: I began by skimming through the latest meteorological reports. Heavy rains were expected to continue over the next 24 hours, and there was no sign of it relenting. The humidity levels were at their peak—saturating the air to the point where each droplet felt heavier, like a promise that the skies were not done yet.

Social Media Updates: I tuned into local social media feeds—WhatsApp groups, Twitter threads, and Facebook communities, all buzzing with live updates. People were posting pictures of flooded roads, stranded vehicles, and waterlogged homes. One post stood out: *"Vishwamitri water levels are reaching danger marks. Will it cross the safety line again like it did in 2005?"*

That question hung in my mind, but I could not afford to dwell on the past. I needed more intel.

Reservoirs and Dams: The trickiest part was understanding what was happening beyond our city's boundaries. If the dams in neighboring states, especially the Sardar Sarovar Dam and the Ajwa Dam were nearing their full capacity, any release of water would feed chaos directly into Vadodara's rivers, creating a surge that could spell disaster for our hotel and of course to a major part of city.

After an hour of diving through government sites and monitoring live feed updates from hydrology centers, I found what I feared: Ajwa's reservoir was inching dangerously close to its brim. They had not announced a release yet, but it was only a matter of time before that decision would be made. And when they did, all that water would inevitably find its way to the Vishwamitri.

The Threat Analysis: The facts were undeniable. We were in the crosshairs of a potential catastrophe. The heavy rainfall in Vadodara, combined with possible upstream dam releases, could push the Vishwamitri to vomit its waters over the banks, spilling into the city, the streets, and quite possibly, into our hotel's premises.

But knowing this was not enough. I needed to devise a plan—a set of protocols and measures to mitigate the impact. As I glanced outside my window at the relentless downpour, a sense of urgency surged within me. I could not wait for the rain to ease. I had to act.

The storm was not just a natural calamity; it was a tactical challenge. And I was ready to engage it head-on.

Chapter - 3

Drawing Battle Lines

The rain hammered against my window with renewed intensity, the relentless downpour roaring like an untamed beast. My eyes, however, were glued to the data streaming in. **212 feet at Ajwa Dam**, **Akota and Mujmahuda bridges crossing the 28-feet mark**—the numbers painted a grim picture. If the rain continued, the Vishwamitri's swelling waters would soon spill over, flooding the city like a tide of chaos.

It was no longer a question of *if* the flood would hit. The real question was *when*.

My phone was already in my hand when I made the decision. "Enough waiting," I thought, "it's time to act."

The first call was to my HR Manager. I spoke in measured tones, giving directives that belied the urgency of the situation. "Get in touch with all our staff and interns staying in low-lying areas," I instructed, "and suggest they move to the hotel premises immediately." The HR Manager's response was a swift, "Yes, sir." But I could hear the underlying concern in his voice.

"Also," I continued, "arrange accommodation for them. Make sure we have enough food and supplies on hand. Ensure their families know they will be safe here, and they will not need to worry."

Within minutes, he was making calls, reaching out to every employee living in flood-prone zones, coordinating with transportation teams to ensure they had a safe way to get to the hotel. It was a logistical feat, but we had done it before in less threatening situations. I knew he would execute it perfectly.

My next call was to the Front Office Manager (FOM). He picked up the call on the first ring, the background noise betraying the hectic energy buzzing through the hotel.

"Do we have rooms available for tonight?" I asked.

"Yes, sir. We have more than enough inventory at the moment," he replied confidently. "Good. Block a room for me. Higher floor, back-facing, overlooking the river."

There was a slight pause at the other end. "Sir?" he questioned, his voice tinged with uncertainty. It was not every day the GM requested a room during a flood warning.

"I need to keep an eye on the Vishwamitri," I clarified. "If the river rises further, I want to see it firsthand."

"Understood, sir," he responded, though the hint of hesitation lingered. I knew he was wondering why I would want a view of the river when it was threatening to breach its banks, but this was not about comfort or aesthetics; it was about readiness.

I needed to position myself right at the heart of the storm's path. It was the best vantage point to assess the threat and plan accordingly.

Chapter - 4

The Call to Action

The time for contemplation had ended. The facts were clear, the river's fury was real, and the threat was no longer a distant possibility. It was time to leave the comforts of home and switch to full combat mode.

Still dressed in casual clothes from my day off, I made the decision. "Pack my greens," I called out to my wife. It was my personal war cry—my code for switching from domestic duty to crisis management. My wife knew exactly what it meant: I was about to step into the storm, no longer a passive observer but an active participant.

As she hurried to pull out the set of dark green attire, I used for situations like these, gear that signified readiness and agility, I took a deep breath, mentally running through the next steps. My role as General Manager was about to take on a new dimension.

I got dressed quickly, slipping into the familiar outfit that felt more like armor than clothing. I grabbed my car keys off the table and almost left for the hotel when a sudden thought struck me. The roads were flooded, underpasses submerged, and water levels unpredictable. Taking my own car in this weather, no matter how capable, seemed like a risk I could not afford.

I dropped the keys back on the table and pulled out my phone again.

"Send a vehicle over to my house," I instructed the front desk. "With a local driver, someone who knows the terrain well." It was a critical detail; someone familiar with the labyrinth of waterlogged streets and alleys would be better equipped to navigate in these treacherous conditions. A local driver would also know which roads were still passable and which had become submerged hazards.

As I hung up the phone, I glanced at the clock. Noon was turning into afternoon, and with each passing minute, the water was rising higher. I stood up, grabbed my essentials, and took one last look around my home.

Then, with a resolve sharpened by the urgency of the situation, I stepped out into the deluge, ready to face the storm head-on.

I was not just going back to the hotel: I was returning to the command center.

The hotel vehicle arrived within fifteen minutes, its headlights cutting through the downpour. I turned to my wife, who had been quietly watching me, her eyes betraying a mix of concern and understanding. I scooped my young daughter Suvira, into my arms, holding her close. "Be good for Mommy," I whispered, placing a gentle kiss on her forehead. She nodded, too young to fully grasp the gravity of the situation but sensing that this was no ordinary departure.

Turning to my wife, I gave her a reassuring look. "Keep all necessary items handy, just in case," I reminded her, though I knew she had already prepared everything. Over the years, we had developed an unspoken understanding in such situations. The departmental store downstairs was well-stocked, and I trusted her to manage things at home if the floods worsened.

I offered quick hugs to my in-laws and a respectful nod to my wife's grandmother '*buddhi,*' as we fondly called her.

"Stay safe, all of you," I said firmly, "and keep an eye on the news."

I lingered for a brief second at the door, absorbing the sight of my home; our haven, one last time. I knew there was a chance I would not be back until the storm subsided, and whatever came, I would be in the thick of it.

"See you all shortly," I said softly, with a mixture of resolve and reassurance in my voice. Then, with a final pat on my wife's shoulder, I stepped out into the deluge, rain cascading down as if the heavens themselves were trying to deter me.

I turned and climbed into the vehicle, my mind already shifting to strategy mode. The driver, a seasoned professional, glanced at me in the rearview mirror, sensing that this ride was going to be different.

"What's your name?" I asked as we pulled out of the lane, rain battering against the windshield.

"Rajesh, sir," he replied confidently.

"Good, Rajesh. You have been driving around the city today, right? Tell me everything you have seen so far where is the water worst? Which roads are completely submerged? Where are the rescue teams already working?"

Rajesh launched into a detailed account, his voice steady despite the tension in the air. He painted a vivid picture of the city's situation: underpasses were filled with water, the old city areas are turning into pools, people abandoned cars on streets as the water level rose too quickly, to escape.

"Ajwa's water levels are making everyone nervous, sir. A lot of people near the riverfront have already started evacuating." *"And the roads leading to the hotel!"* I interrupted. "The route we are taking now is the only one still open, but even it is getting bad."

I nodded, absorbing every word. Rajesh's firsthand knowledge filled in the gaps that the data alone could not cover. He knew which areas were suffering most and which neighborhoods were at the brink of being swallowed by the floods. With each turn, his commentary added another layer to my understanding of the demographic threat approaching the hotel.

We drove past submerged under-bridges and waterlogged streets, the entire landscape of the city transforming into a murky, treacherous scene. This was not just a ride; it was reconnaissance.

The drive to the hotel was tense. Even with the local driver expertly navigating through partially flooded streets, there was a palpable sense of foreboding in the air. As we approached the familiar outline of the hotel, a surge of adrenaline shot through me. This was no longer just a place of work—it was ground zero.

The staff I had called earlier were waiting near the entrance, their faces a reflection of both relief and concern as they saw me arrive. I stepped out of the vehicle, scanning the hotel grounds and surrounding areas. The Vishwamitri was still holding back, but for how long?

I glanced back at Rajesh. "You've given me more information in this short ride than hours of reports could," I said, gratitude seeping into my voice. "Stay safe and keep sharing updates with the front desk if you see anything new."

He nodded, offering a slight smile before driving off.

As I walked into the hotel, rain-soaked but resolute, I knew one thing for certain: I had gained a crucial ally in the form of Rajesh's eyes and ears on the ground.

As I looked up at the stormy sky, the weight of responsibility settled squarely on my shoulders. I was not just stepping into a building—I was stepping into the heart of the crisis. The battle had begun.

Chapter - 5

A Long Night of Vigilance and Uncertainty

The crisis that loomed over Vadodara was not anomalous. Just fifteen days ago, the city had faced a similar threat, though less intense. Back then, the waters had teased the boundaries of danger, but the municipal authorities managed to avert disaster at the last moment. This time, I hoped they would act swiftly and decisively to save the city from plunging into chaos once again.

But mere hope was not enough, rather it was a mirage!

The evening sky darkened as rain continued to cascade relentlessly, and I knew the worst might still be ahead. I slipped into full operation mode, making rounds of the entire property to assess the potential impact of direct rainfall. Walking through the lobby, the kitchens, the basement—every corridor and every hall, my eyes darted, rolled and scrolled from ceiling to floor, searching for any sign of leakage, seepage, or structural vulnerability.

The wind howled outside, and the news from the city was anything but not reassuring. Updates came pouring in like the rain: the usual suspects, low-lying areas were already submerged. For the residents there, flooding was almost a ritual, something that happened twice a year like an unwanted ceremony. I could almost picture them stacking their furniture higher, resigned to the cruel familiarity of water invading their homes.

My rounds extended into the evening. The sound of rain pounding against the windows and rooftops was accompanied by the persistent ping of my phone. Updates kept rolling in, the status checks, requests for information, and worst of all, cancellations. Event bookings for the day were falling through one by one, and incoming guests were calling to cancel their reservations.

But my focus was forked. While I analyzed the potential business loss, I was also managing the resources needed to keep the property operational. High-speed diesel (HSD) for our generators was a top priority. I made sure our stock would last through the night and that was to be situation no matter what.

Meanwhile, the team was working tirelessly. Housekeeping was providing extra amenities to the guests and staff who had shifted in, the kitchen team was preparing meals to keep everyone comfortable, and security was keeping watch on the outside premises, making sure there were no hazardous obstructions or overflowing drains.

Every member of the staff was on their toes, and we moved like a well-coordinated unit. I walked through the lobby, passing the young interns who had taken refuge in the hotel. They looked relieved but also apprehensive. I stopped to speak with a few of them, offering a word of assurance.

"Do not worry. You are safe here. And your families know you are well cared for."

I saw some nods of appreciation and even a few smiles. It was a small gesture, but in situations like these, morale matters as much as preparation does. The sense of duty kept me on my feet, checking and rechecking every aspect of the property. If the rain did not let up, we would be dealing with more than just comfort; we would be looking at the safety of everyone inside.

The hours slipped by, and the constant monitoring had me shifting between screens filled with monsoon data, live river levels, dam status reports, and our hotel's business records. My mind felt like a machine with gears whirring in constant motion, but I could not afford to stop. The stakes were too high.

Late into the night, I called for a final team meeting in the staff lounge. Faces that were tired but resolute turned towards me as I addressed them.

"We've managed well so far, but we don't know what tomorrow holds," I began, my voice steady. "I need each of you to stay vigilant. Keep a close eye on all guests' needs, any possible threats and on every corner of the property. Let us be prepared for whatever comes. And remember—if the Vishwamitri overflows, we are the first line of defense here. We are not just protecting our property; we are ensuring the safety and wellbeing of everyone inside."

There were nods of understanding, shoulders straightening with determination. I thanked them all for their efforts and dismissed the team, urging them to rest where they could.

As I finally made my way to my room, exhaustion began to weigh down on me, but I pushed it aside. I had picked a room facing the back, overlooking the river, specifically for moments like this. I stood by the window, staring at the ominous silhouette of the Vishwamitri below, trying to gauge its threat in the darkness.

I glanced at my phone one last time, refreshing the hydrology department's live feed. The water levels were inching closer to the danger mark, but the updates were sporadic now, hinting at the possibility of a dam release.

With a deep breath, I turned away from the window, knowing I had done all I could for the day. There would be no rest tonight, not really. I slipped off my shoes, lay back on the bed, and closed my eyes, my mind still mapping out scenarios and responses.

Tomorrow would be a different kind of challenge, but at least, for now, we were ready for it.

Chapter - 6

Awakening the Warrior Within

After hours of relentless vigilance and calculations, exhaustion finally took hold. My body gave in to the weight of weariness as I sank into the comfort of the hotel room bed. For a brief moment, I found myself in the lap of deep slumber—a rare solace amidst the chaos.

But then it happened. A voice pierced through the stillness, loud and sharp, slicing through the fog of sleep. ***"Are you sleeping?"***

I jolted awake, my heart pounding, every muscle tensed, eyes wide and searching the room. There was no one. No figure standing in the shadows, no intruder, no staff member calling for help. Just the steady hum of the air conditioner and the distant patter of rain against the window.

And then I smiled. It was not an external voice; it was my own. The inner voice that always kept me sharp and ready, the voice that roused me to confront challenges head-on, or sometimes, miraculously, offered solutions to seemingly impossible problems in my sleep. It was like having a second mind that worked tirelessly even when I rested.

Call it uncanny, call it eerie, but I had come to accept it as part of who I was. The voice had awakened me countless times before, giving me that sudden flash of insight; the missing piece of a puzzle, the breakthrough idea, or simply a jolt of energy that reinvigorated me when I needed it most. And tonight, it reminded me that the fight was far from over.

My pulse slowed back to normal, but I was wide awake, my senses crackling with alertness: as if I had just chugged a can of taurine-infused energy drink. There was no going back to sleep now. I reached for my phone and checked the latest updates from the hydrology department. The water levels were still rising, and each update showed an inching increase, feeding the river's menace.

The numbers on my screen were a stark reminder that we were on the brink of a critical moment. With each new reading, I felt myself transforming, evolving from the steady, composed General Manager into a war commander on high alert. The river was our adversary, and we were about to enter its battlefield.

I sat up, eyes flickering between screens and messages, refreshing the dam statistics compulsively. Ajwa was now teetering at 214 feet, dangerously close to the overflow mark. The reservoirs upstream showed no sign of respite. They were feeding into each other like a chain reaction, and if even one dam released its waters, the Vishwamitri would surge through the city like a marauding beast, drowning and destroying everything in its path.

The night dragged on, but there was no sense of time anymore, only an unrelenting state of awareness. Outside, the rain pounded in steady sheets, blurring the world beyond my window. The city was sleeping or was trying to! oblivious to the slow-moving calamity inching closer.

At exactly 5 a.m., I hit the screenshot button, capturing the grim numbers on my screen, and shared it with the Heads of Departments group. The image spoke louder than words. Ajwa Dam at **214 feet**.

There was no need for explanations or clarifications. My team knew what that meant. The floodgates were practically at their breaking point. As the first rays of dawn began to seep through the heavy clouds, casting a muted light over the city, I could see the responses rolling in. Short acknowledgments, crisp affirmations. My team was awake and ready.

I rose from the bed, my muscles tense but my mind sharper than ever. No longer just the General Manager of a luxury hotel, I had become the frontline strategist, planning, executing, and anticipating every possible outcome. I started getting dressed, slipping back into my "greens," as I responded to a slew of messages and emails that had piled up overnight.

Operations must continue as usual, the guests were still checking in and out, events had to be cancelled or rescheduled, and a dozen other minor crises were brewing on the side. I could not neglect any of it. Despite the looming threat, the show had to go on. We could not declare a state of emergency until our adversary, the Vishwamitri, did so itself.

Until then, we were in a paradoxical state; hyper-prepared yet pretending everything was normal. It was like playing chess with an unseen opponent, where one wrong move could lead to a checkmate.

The air felt heavy as I stepped out of the room, fully geared up for the day ahead. The calm before the storm was not just a phrase, it was rather a palpable sensation. The hotel buzzed with activity as staff moved swiftly, preparing for a day that promised to be anything but ordinary.

And as I headed downstairs, I felt that familiar surge of determination, that inner voice whispering again, not as a scream this time but as a steady, unwavering reminder:

Be ready. It's coming.

And I was.

Chapter - 7

Navigating the Storm's Chaos

The atmosphere in the meeting room was thick with tension as I gathered all Heads of Departments for our emergency meeting. We were facing an unprecedented challenge, and every moment counted. With heavy rain still pouring outside, the urgency of the situation weighed on our shoulders.

I kicked off the meeting with a stern but determined tone. "We need to execute our action plan immediately. The latest updates indicate that Akota Road, the main access route from the railway station and bus stand, is completely waterlogged. Vehicles are struggling to make it through. Our operations could be severely affected if we do not act quickly."

As I scanned the room, my heart sank at the realization that we were already short-staffed. The absence of three key Heads of Departments loomed over us like a dark cloud. Our Chief Engineer resigned recently, and the newly appointed one would not be joining us for another fortnight. I had hoped to navigate the situation with the existing team, but now that seemed increasingly difficult.

"Where's our Executive Housekeeper?" I asked, bracing myself for the answer.

I was informed that the route from his residence was submerged. I knew how vital his presence was, especially with the influx of guests and the urgent need for housekeeping services in this situation.

Turning my attention to the HR Manager, I asked, "What about HR?"

I picked up the phone to speak with the HR Manager, he immediately picked up the call and answered in one breath, "Sir, I am at the police barricade right now. They are not allowing anyone to pass through," said the HR Manager who was on the other side of the barricade. "Listen," I said, my voice steady despite the circumstances. "Do not take any risks. Follow the instructions from local authorities. We will manage without you for now."

This left me without the presence of any HR manager in the hotel. The HR Manager was running the department alone with the help of just an intern, and now that responsibility too was entirely on me.

As I continued to gather information, I discovered that many senior members of the housekeeping team were also stranded in their respective localities or on the way, unable to report to duty. The ripple effects of the flood were spreading throughout the hotel, impacting every department. I had requested many team members to stay back at the hotel, especially those who lived alone, but reality had proven unforgiving.

The absence of three critical HODs—one responsible for engineering, second for people and the other for housekeeping—was a significant setback. I was already aware that I would need to step in for the engineering functions, but I had not anticipated how much the lack of leadership would hinder our response.

To add to the complications, a few months ago, our stores in-charge—who had been with us for last twelve years—left the organization for better opportunities. And his assistant, while resourceful, was only capable of managing the routine tasks. This meant we were short on hands for critical supplies and materials' inventory management as well.

I took a deep breath, trying to recalibrate my thoughts. "Alright, we're facing challenges, but we have to work with what we've got," I said, my voice firm. "Let us prioritize our resources. Engineering will be my focus for now. I will oversee any technical issues that arise."

The room buzzed with a sense of urgency as I turned to the remaining department heads. "Housekeeping team needs to ensure we maintain essential cleanliness in public areas, especially with our guests coming in. We must keep the hotel running smoothly despite the circumstances."

The team nodded; their determination rekindled. I could see them rising to the challenge, fueled by a shared sense of responsibility.

"We also need a communication strategy," I continued. "I need a log of all staff who are stranded and unable to reach the hotel ask them if they are safe at their places. Ensure those who are here have the resources they need to stay comfortable."

"Lastly," I added, glancing at the clock, "stay updated on any new reports from the city. The municipal authorities may issue evacuation notices, and we need to be prepared for anything."

With that, I wrapped up the meeting, feeling the weight of our challenges but also a spark of resilience within the team. We had our plan, albeit a shaky one, but it was a plan, nonetheless. As everyone dispersed, I felt determination in the room and knew we could weather this storm together.

Stepping back into the hotel corridor, I could hear various people talking about the routes to reach the airport or railway station. I told myself that I would need to be vigilant and adaptable in the coming hours. The Vishwamitri might be rising, but we were ready to rise with it; our collective strength would not waver.

We were in this together, and together we would navigate through the chaos.

Chapter - 8

The Deceptive Calm

Although the day had dawned differently and there was no torrential downpour, no ominous rumble of clouds overhead. Instead, there was an unusual stillness, the sky a confusing mix of hazy clouds with patches of fleeting sunlight. It was a sight that would have given a naive observer some misplaced hope that the worst was behind us.

But deep down, I knew better. The lull was unnerving, a deceptive calm that often preluded something far more formidable. Having seen nature's unpredictable fury over the years, I knew this momentary pause was merely the eye of the storm or an interlude before chaos reigned again.

I decided to take a round of the hotel premises, my eyes scanning every inch for signs of potential vulnerabilities. It was crucial to remain vigilant; the exterior periphery, the drainage points, and the generator setups were inspected once again. Everything had to be perfect. The comforting routine of these checks helped me gather my thoughts and reaffirm our preparedness.

I walked out onto the porch, the familiar feeling of anticipation settling into my bones. The road in front of the hotel, which usually buzzed with the activity of cars, bikes, and pedestrians, was strangely sparse. A few vehicles passed by cautiously, navigating the damp and slippery roads with care. The erratic nature of the traffic mirrored the indecisiveness of the skies above, as if everyone were bracing themselves for something.

My mind wandered as I stared at the road. This calm before the storm made me restless. It felt like a carefully laid trap, a subtle misdirection meant to lull us into lowering our guard. My focus was broken by a cheerful voice behind me.

"Boss, baarish toh nahi ho raha ab, baad nahi aayega, right?" ("Boss, it's not raining anymore, so there will be no floods"!) It was one of our bell boys, his voice brimming with innocent optimism. He was a young lad, new to the world of managing crises, and his hopeful demeanor was almost endearing. He had been working with me for a while now and had seen me tackle challenges head-on.

I turned to him and smiled, a faint one, knowing that his words were born out of genuine belief rather than naivety. *"Yahan jitna paani barasna tha baras gaya,"* ("The water which has poured in here was enough") I said, keeping my tone light. *"Ab jahan se paani beh ke aayega, wahan ka mausam dekhna padega."* ("Now we will have to worry about the weather of the places from where the flooding water will originate") My words carried the truth he might not have grasped yet and the threat was not just the local rain, but the rivers and reservoirs upstream were more dangerous.

The bell boy nodded, still holding onto his sense of relief. He grinned, eyes twinkling with a childlike trust as he added, *"Aap ho toh kya darr hai, aap sab handle kar lenge."* ("Why should we fear when you are there, you will handle everything"). There was no flattery or pretense in his tone. He said it with pure, unvarnished sincerity.

For a moment, I stood there, absorbing his words. He was there during the floods of 2019, when we had managed to keep the hotel safe from the water's clutches. He had seen me lead the team through those challenging days, rallying everyone to push back the encroaching floodwaters and prevent the hotel from becoming waterlogged. I realized then that his faith was not just in me as his boss, but in the collective spirit we had built over the years.

"Thank you," I said softly, watching him as he disappeared into the lobby, his back straight with newfound confidence. I knew he meant every word. He genuinely believed that if I were there, we would weather this storm too.

But his words did more than offering encouragement, they also served as a stark reminder of the responsibility I bore. The team, the guests, and even the city were looking at us, expecting us to be a beacon of safety. We were no longer just a hotel. In these situations, we became a sanctuary, a place people could turn to when the world outside seemed determined to break down every barrier.

I felt the weight of their expectations settle on my shoulders, and with it, a renewed sense of determination. It was not about feeling fear or uncertainty, instead it was about leading through it. I had to be vigilant, to keep anticipating, preparing, and acting before any crisis turned into disaster.

I took a deep breath, turning my gaze back to the still road. The calmness was unsettling, almost mocking in its deceit. I knew better than to trust it. Just because the rain had paused did not mean we were in the clear.

"Stay alert," I murmured to myself. The bell boy's unwavering faith would not be betrayed. With that, I walked back inside, the comforting ambience of the hotel's operations buzzing around me. There was work to be done and precious little time to do it in.

The morning might have been quiet, but I knew the storm was far from over.

Chapter - 9

Battling Time and the Unseen Surge

It was 10 a.m., and the city had no electricity since morning, kind of an expected bane considering the nightmarish scenario unfolding in other parts of Vadodara. The rhythmic humming of our diesel generator continued as a steady reminder of the fragile state of affairs. The generator's low rumble was not just a noise; it was an alarm of sorts, signaling that the city was teetering on the edge. Power was evidently down in many areas, and our hotel, perched on a precarious strip near the swollen Vishwamitri, stood as an island of light in an ocean of looming darkness.

I had been keeping a vigilant watch over the river level from the terrace, my eyes trained on the subtle rise and fall of the water like a seasoned sailor scanning the horizon for the slightest change. I also monitored Akota Road, which acted like a gauge for us, the barometer that would indicate when the real trouble was set to begin. I knew the behavior of the river during floods too well, it's erratic tendencies and merciless flooding pattern.

Having observed two major floods in the past, I had mapped out an eerie understanding of how the river would creep into the city. It would not begin here at the hotel's entrance or through the front roads. Rather, it would first seep into the back portion of Samrajya Society, the massive residential complex sprawling right beside us. Like an insidious serpent, the water would slither through its narrow alleys and rear entrance, quietly establishing its territory before striking with full force.

After a brief respite and a cup of tea that did little to calm my nerves, I gathered the managers and HODs. It was time to brief them, not just on operational protocol but on the very nature of the threat we faced. I found myself explaining the peculiar behavior of the river, drawing parallels with past events and detailing how the water would infiltrate the drainage systems, creating a cascade of failures across the city's infrastructure.

"Stay focused," I reiterated. "We are not just battling rain; we are dealing with a river that does not care about boundaries. It is essential to anticipate where the water might reach and when."

My eyes shifted around the group as I asked each of them about their own living situations. It was not just professional preparedness that mattered right now; it was personal safety. I wanted to know if anyone's family or property was in immediate danger and whether we needed to bring more people into the hotel for refuge.

One by one, they shared their locations, and I mentally noted the threat levels. To my relief, I learned that the Executive Housekeeper, who was stuck at his residence due to waterlogged roads, was in a relatively safe locality, and his landlord, an older, vigilant gentleman; was also present at home. A sigh of relief escaped me; at least, he was not in imminent danger.

I then turned to the Executive Chef, a pillar of our food production team. He hesitated for a moment before stating his address, which was not far from the hotel. His question, however, reflected the anxiety that was gripping all of us.

"Aapko kya lagta hai sir, wahan paani aaega?" ("In your opinion, will it be flooding there?") he asked softly, concerned lacing his voice.

Flooded Floors to Open Doors: A Sanctuary Reclaimed

I glanced up at the sky, almost as if seeking guidance from a higher power. There was no easy answer to give. I had been recommending that those in vulnerable areas bring their families to the hotel, but his place was in a grey zone not at risk, but not entirely safe either.

"Follow up with me in exactly 30 minutes," I instructed, trying to buy some time to assess the situation further. "And remember, it's always better to be a little more prepared every time." My voice carried a weight which I hoped conveyed the seriousness of the decision he needed to make.

While he nodded, I realized there was another critical task I had to check on. The generator had been humming like a powerful beast, flaunting its prowess and indispensability for quite some time now. Vadodara rarely experiences power outages, and the DG set usually ran more on routine tests than in actual usage. Today, however, it was our unsung hero, a 320 KVA machine that was keeping the hotel's heart beating.

I marched over to the generator room, my footsteps were brisk. As I reached, I pointed at the empty HSD barrels and instructed Manu, our engineering supervisor, to siphon out whatever fuel was left in the filled barrels and pour it into the DG's reservoir tank. "We need all barrels refilled and stocked up," I commanded. If the power outage persisted for longer than anticipated, running out of diesel would plunge us into complete darkness, compounding the crisis.

As I moved around, directing tasks and getting things aligned, a sudden thought hit me. "Where's Raju?" I asked, referring to the store assistant I had sent out earlier for rainwater pipes.

"Sir, abhi baat hua hai. Thoda time lagega. Aa hi raha hai," ("Sir we just spoke, he will take little time, but he is on the way") Manu replied nonchalantly.

The word 'time' echoed like a drum in my ears. *Time*. It was the one luxury we did not have.

A surge of adrenaline shot through me as I remembered the Chef. "Wait," I said aloud, startling Manu. "The Chef was supposed to follow up with me. Why didn't he?"

I immediately dialed his number. The line connected, and I did not wait for pleasantries. *"Chef, tum mujhse follow up lene waale they, paanch minute zyada ho gaya. Call kyun nahi kiya?"* ("Chef you were supposed to take follow up with me in half hour, its 5 minute up than that, why didn't you call"?) My tone was stern, almost reprimanding.

"Sir, main call karne hi wala tha..." ("sir I was about to call") he stammered, a sheepish grin evident even over the phone.

"No excuses," I interrupted, my voice firm but laced with concern. *"Chef, tumhara ghar paas mein hi hai. Aur tumhare paas bas tees minute ka time hai. Jaldi jao aur family ko leke aao. Agar 30 minutes mein nahin sab kiya, toh phir kuch nahi kar paoge. Yahan tab tak main sambhalta hoon."* ("Chef your house is nearby, you have 30 minutes, go running and bring your family here, ensure to complete the task in half hour, else it will be too late. I will take care of the things here.")

I could almost hear the wheels in his head turning the mental calculus of what it would take to ensure his family's safety while ensuring he could still return to the hotel. His home was just two minutes away, but with a young child that too a toddler, collecting essential items could take much longer.

With a brisk acknowledgment, he hung up, and I knew he was already on his way. I pivoted back to Manu, mentally cycling through the next set of tasks we needed to get done.

Time was becoming a relentless adversary, slipping through my fingers like the river water itself. Each minute ticking away was another moment closer to uncertainty.

"Manu," I said, my voice unwavering. "We need to finalize the plan for utilities and pumps. I want every contingency covered. Make sure all backup systems are operational and ready to switch at a moment's notice."

He nodded, and we set about our tasks, a flurry of movement and urgency, each step guided by the knowledge that the calm outside was fleeting. The Vishwamitri was biding its time, and when it finally decided to strike, we had to be prepared to face its wrath.

Every second mattered now; both in safeguarding the hotel and ensuring that the people under our roof were safe. The bell boy's innocent faith, the Chef's hurried preparations, and Manu's diligent work, all hinged on our ability to stay one step ahead of the flood.

This was more than just a logistical battle. It was a race against time, a struggle to outmaneuver nature itself. And the clock was ticking faster than ever.

Chapter - 10

The Unsettling Harbinger

The signs of impending disaster were everywhere, subtle yet unmistakable. The once-busy street outside the hotel, typically bustling with honking cars and city traffic, had taken on an eerie stillness. Slowly but steadily, the fancy sedans and SUVs were replaced by rugged tractors and high-axle vehicles, the kind that only come out when wading through knee-deep water becomes a necessity. It was as if the city's pulse had slowed down, gearing up for a quiet resignation to the chaos that was sure to follow.

I stood at the entrance, my eyes darting between the vehicles and the innocuous patch of ground outside the hotel where the municipal corporation's underground drain line lay buried deep beneath. Only someone who knew where to look could spot it—a concealed; heavy metal grill chamber lid hidden so skillfully that passersby would never guess at the drainage system lying below. Yet, for me, it was a focal point of anxiety.

The water level in the concealed chamber had been rising at a disconcerting pace. What started as a slow trickle had become a steady, determined swell. I could see ripples forming under the grate, like subtle tremors before a quake. Each inch the water climbed sent a new wave of calculations spinning in my mind. I envisioned the underground labyrinth of drain lines crisscrossing the city, all of them leading here, converging like tributaries feeding a deadly river.

The magnitude of what was about to happen was dawning on me, layer by layer, with every glance at that underground chamber. And just as I was turning away, heading toward the time office to tally the staff who had made it in, I caught a flash of movement out of the corner of my eye.

Something winged, fast, and utterly repugnant darted across my path. My heart skipped a beat as I spun around. "Wait... what was that?" I murmured under my breath. My gaze locked on it for a brief second, then I muttered again, "Was that... an American cockroach?"

A wave of unease washed over me. Seeing one of those monstrous cockroaches, pale brown, long antennae twitching as it scuttled across the floor. It was not just disgusting; it was like a sudden, unwelcome reminder of hidden dangers lurking below. The appearance of an American cockroach, especially in an upscale establishment like ours, was not a pest control issue. It was an omen.

These roaches were not your average pests. They are known to inhabit sewers and drainpipes, thriving in the dark, humid recesses of city underbellies. For one to appear here, in broad daylight, meant one thing, that the floodwaters were invading their subterranean homes, forcing them to abandon ship and swarm dry areas.

My skin prickled with the realization. It was akin to seeing enemy warplanes invading a no- fly zone; silent, sinister, and undeniable proof that the worst was about to come. If the roaches were coming up, it meant the water levels in the neighboring areas were rising, filling up the drains and pushing these creatures out of their lairs. The unseen chaos below the surface was starting to spill over, and this was just the beginning.

As if on cue, I spotted another one, skittering towards a dry corner. My jaw tightened. This was more than just an isolated incident. It was the harbinger of something unstoppable, a prelude to the havoc that was gearing up to break loose at any moment.

Taking a deep breath, I fought the urge to stamp out the vile creature, knowing full well that this was a battle we could not win with mere brute force. I needed to remain calm, think, and strategize. These roaches were messengers, not the real threat. They were warning me, in their grotesque manner, that the underground drain lines of the surrounding neighborhoods were swelling beyond capacity.

I turned on my heel and headed straight back to the lobby, a new urgency propelling my steps. I needed to recheck the status of the lower basement and the main utility areas. If the water pressure forced its way into our drainage system, it would not take long before it found an entry point, weak or otherwise, and then it would be a battle to keep the hotel's foundation from turning into a swamp.

Passing by the housekeeping staff, I motioned them to gather nearby. "Listen, team," I began, my voice clipped and intense. "I need all potential entry points, drain covers, pipeline vents, and utility shafts to be sealed off immediately. Stuff them with anything you can find. If we leave even a single gap, the water and everything else will get in.

Understood?"

They nodded, catching the gravity of my words. I could see their expressions changing from confusion to comprehension. They knew before something was off; now they knew just how serious it was.

Leaving them to the task, I grabbed my phone and dialed Manu. "Manu, we've got a new problem," I said curtly as soon as he answered. "I just saw a couple of American roaches near the time office. That means the water's starting to force them out of the drains. Check the basement and the back areas for any signs of backflow or seepage."

"On it, sir," he replied, his voice steady.

The next few hours were going to be critical. If we could pre-emptively plug in every potential entry, we might stand a chance. But the cockroaches had already sounded the alarm. The city's underbelly was preparing to vomit out everything it could no longer hold. And as I stood in the hallway, watching the staff scramble to carry out the orders, I could not shake the feeling that we were being slowly, inexorably surrounded.

The war had not just begun—it was already halfway to our doorstep.

Chapter - 11

Holding the Fort Amidst the Rising Tide

As the clock ticked closer to mid-morning, the controlled chaos of the hotel's operations was beginning to blur the line between normalcy and a looming state of emergency. Every person on the floor was moving with an unspoken urgency, fueled by a mixture of anxiety and duty. From duty managers coordinating guest movements to the housekeeping staff sprinting from room to room; every soul was in a state of hyper-focus. Yet, amidst all this, a sense of disbelief lingered in the air, as if some still hoped that the deluge would miraculously change course, leaving us dry and unaffected.

I glanced over to the reception area and saw our Front Office Manager (FOM) pacing back and forth, his face flushed with agitation. Just a few hours ago, he had been amused by my safety precautions for the staff and had casually brushed off the situation as something manageable. But now, his expression told a different story. His phone buzzed incessantly, and every time he answered, the lines on his forehead deepened.

Unable to ignore the shift in his demeanor, I walked over and caught his eye. "What's going on?" I asked calmly, though I already had an inkling.

"My wife just called. She says the water is starting to rise in our locality," he stammered, a faint tremor in his voice. There was no trace of the nonchalance he had displayed earlier. "I told them to come to the hotel when you suggested it in the morning, but they did not take it seriously. Now, look at what is happening..." he trailed off, sounding both angry and helpless.

I placed a firm hand on his shoulder, making him look at me. "There's still time," I said, my tone steady but insistent. "Do not waste another second. Run. Get our hotel car and bring them here. Now."

For a split second, he hesitated, caught in the irony of how swiftly things had turned. Then, as if jolted into action, he nodded, grabbed the car keys, and sprinted out of the lobby. I watched him disappear into the rain-drenched street, silently hoping he would not be too late.

Turning back, I took stock of the situation. The Duty Managers were on high alert, juggling guest inquiries and logistical challenges. Guests were growing restless and agitated as the waterlogged city threw their travel plans into disarray. Many had missed flights or had their train journeys cancelled due to impassable roads. Some were checking back in, realizing their homes were no safer than the submerged streets.

The team had switched into crisis management mode. They were trying to contact local transport agencies and find alternate routes for guests to reach the airport or railway station. Meanwhile, the housekeeping team was working tirelessly to prepare rooms for these unexpected check-ins. Although understaffed, their dedication made every person seem like a small battalion of their own. They were turning over rooms, cleaning public areas, and ensuring guests had all the amenities they needed, as if nothing were amiss.

I reached for the phone and dialed the Food and Beverage Manager (FBM). When he answered, his voice was remarkably calm. "Sir, everything is under control on our end. We are running the kitchen as per schedule and catering to all orders."

"How's your family?" I asked, wanting to ensure the well-being of the very people supporting the operation.

"They are fine, sir. We live on the first floor, and even if the water rises, we have moved everything important to higher shelves. There is no immediate concern," he replied. I could hear the strength in his words and a deep sense of preparedness that brought a brief smile to my face.

"Good. Now, make sure we have backup stores for the kitchen and enough dry ingredients shifted to the highest racks. And see if we can relocate some of the linen stock to safer areas, just in case."

"Yes, sir. I will get it done right away," he assured me before hanging up.

I turned my attention back to the lobby, where a new wave of guests was making their way in, some with suitcases hastily packed, others with just a few essentials. Many were locals who lived in low-lying areas now designated as red zones. I spotted the FOM returning with his family, guiding them through the entrance as they hurriedly brushed off droplets of rainwater caused by a brief drizzle. Relief was evident on his face, but I could also see his sense of duty kicking back in.

I approached him, meeting his gaze with a knowing nod. "Welcome back. There are many locals trying to check in right now. Please make sure they are attended to and reassured.

Also, keep printing a new guest list after every check-in, and cross-reference it with the list of vacant, dirty, and occupied rooms."

"Yes, sir," he responded, with a new determination in his voice.

"Do not worry about the back end right now. We have gotten that covered. Focus on the guests— they need to feel like we are in control," I added.

He nodded, already flipping through the front desk log to align his team. It was amazing to see how quickly everyone was adapting. In moments like these, the true spirit of hospitality, of serving, comforting, and leading remarkably, shines through. Despite the growing uncertainty and the mounting tension, every team member seemed to have tapped into a hidden reservoir of resilience.

For a moment, I stood back, watching the entire operation unfold. The concierge, bellhops, and receptionists moved with a grace and efficiency that belied the underlying panic. The kitchen continued churning out orders like clockwork, and the housekeepers flitted about the floors, tidying and prepping rooms as if welcoming new guests was the sole priority.

Everyone was pulling double duty. The absence of several senior staff members and the understaffed departments could have easily caused a breakdown. But instead, it felt as though every person had transformed into an extension of someone else. They were making up for the absences with their sheer willpower and unbreakable spirit.

The situation outside was getting grimmer, yet inside the hotel, a kind of steadfast calm reigned. I watched as the FOM coordinated the influx of local guests seeking refuge, ushering them in with reassuring smiles and providing constant updates on room availability and alternate routes.

It was as if the hotel had become an island, a fortress against the rising tide, and every one of us was a sentinel standing guard, prepared to face whatever came next. The storm might rage on, but we were determined to hold our ground, shoulder to shoulder, until the very last wave crashed against us.

The day was far from over, and with each passing minute, we were bracing for the unknown. But one thing was clear: we were ready to meet it head-on, with an unwavering attitude and an unflinching spirit.

Chapter - 12

The First Breach

I knew the modus operandi of the river. My past experiences had equipped me with a detailed mental map of its wrath, how it swells, how it meanders, and most crucially, how it breaches its boundaries. I had seen it all before. Because of these insights, I was aware that the river could, at its worst, engulf up to 3 feet of my lower basement. If that happened, it would be the worst flood Vadodara had ever seen. According to my calculations, most of Samrajya Society would be submerged under water, and many reputed hotels and commercial complexes would have knee-deep water in their lobbies. *Civic authorities cannot be so naïve in their calculations,* I murmured to myself, though a gnawing doubt still lingered.

As I was making these mental calculations, I noticed something that made my heart skip a beat, it was a feeble stream of water trickling from the entry gate, slowly making its way toward the hotel. The sight of it was like watching an uninvited guest walk through your door unannounced.

"This is just the beginning," I thought, grabbing a water wiper from the corner. I barked instructions to my team, "Make sure all this water goes to the rainwater chamber in the lower basement. It should not head toward the ground floor parking. Otherwise, it will seep into the wells of the elevator." The urgency in my voice was palpable.

Without a second thought, we began pushing the water towards the ramp that led to the rainwater chamber. The ramp acted as a small channel, funneling the water toward the chamber that I had already equipped with two rainwater pumps and a mud pump, ready for action.

Simultaneously, items in the lower basement were being stacked at a height of six feet and above. The thought lingered in the back of my mind: *May God forbid, if the flood comes with full vengeance, at least our essentials will be safe.*

The FOM had already started shifting computers and other necessary items from the admin office to the lobby. Meanwhile, the bellhop took charge of transferring items from my office. There was a sense of unity and purpose that pulsated through the team, as if we were part of a well-rehearsed drill. Yet, with every movement, I could feel the anxiety creeping up in everyone's eyes.

With a little force, but with a lot of determination, we kept pushing the water, redirecting it away from vulnerable areas. As the water began to accumulate inside the premises, I instinctively began recollecting every bit of information I had gathered over the years, the water levels from previous floods, the pressure points in the building, the weak spots in the vicinity. I started matching this data with the new situation unfolding before me. While I processed it all, I was also calling and giving marching orders to my team, one after another.

"Manu, make sure the mud pump is set up in the lower basement! bring out the wipers from the housekeeping storage and get more buckets from the kitchen!" My voice rang out like a commander on the battlefield, directing troops amidst cannon fire.

With every additional stream of water that snaked its way into our territory, the stakes grew higher. Yet, the energy that reverberated through us was one of steadfastness. My team, despite fatigued, undermanned, and up against an unpredictable adversary, still moved with a precision that spoke volumes about their commitment.

In that moment, I knew: the war had now officially begun. The river had made its first breach, but we were ready. Ready to defend our fort, no matter what happens.

Chapter - 13

Nature's Ballet: When the City Dances with the Moon

Every city has its rhythms, its own pulse. But when a flood hits, it is as if all these rhythms align and clash at once, creating a chaos that is terrifyingly beautiful. It is not just the rain that dictates the flow of water; the city's very infrastructure becomes a player in this unruly symphony. *City, drainages, rivers, sea, and moon: they all dance to a particular tune when it comes to floods.* Each element pulls and pushes in its own way, affecting the others in a delicate, yet disruptive, balance.

When it rains, the soil drinks up as much water as it can, saturating itself like a sponge. Whatever remains begins its journey through the veins of the city, *the drainage systems*. These drains are the lifelines that connect to the rivers, and the rivers, in turn, find their destiny in the sea. Under normal circumstances, it is a seamless transition, just like a perfect chain of command where every drop of water knows its place.

But floods defy this order. When water levels rise and the drains can no longer keep up, that is when the delicate equilibrium shatters. The level of the drainage system needs to stay at a higher altitude, serving as a tributary that feeds into the river. However, the moment there is an exact match between the levels of the river and the drainage system, an uncanny state of equilibrium is achieved. At this point, no matter how much water is poured into the drains, it will not flow; it will only stagnate.

Yet, nature's fury does not stop at equilibrium. As the level of the river continues to rise, so do the levels in the drains, and the balance tips over to a dangerous side. This is when the drains, rather than carrying away water, start acting as feeders. The sumps and the *'underworld'* hidden beneath sewer holes and grates, begin to swell and rise. What was once a simple drain is now becoming a menacing fountain, ready to erupt. Sewer holes start rattling and then open up, and what used to be a place for rainwater to disappear into, suddenly becomes a geyser, sending water back onto the roads, into homes, and onto hotel premises.

The river's final refuge is the sea, but the sea, too, has its moods. The sea's willingness to swallow the river depends on its own state of being, *'the tides'* dictated by the whims of the moon. During a full moon, the sea grows hungry with high tides, refusing to accept the river's gift. And, coincidentally, we were just two days away from a full moon. It was like standing at the edge of a battlefield, fully aware that the cavalry; *'the tides'* manipulated by the moon, would soon join in, making an already unpredictable situation even more volatile.

The theory might sound academic, like something out of a textbook. But every bit of it mattered. Every calculation I made was not just to measure the scale of the chaos but to understand its duration and predict its next move.

"All these volumes of water will stop till where? And till when?" That was the real question. Chaos might be inevitable but knowing when it would peak and when it would subside was crucial. It gave me a semblance of control in a situation where everything was slipping through my fingers like the very water I was fighting against.

This was not just about drains overflowing or a river surging beyond its capacity. This was about understanding a whole choreography of nature, *the one* that involved not just the rains or the river but the sea and even the moon. As the minutes turned into hours, I knew every drop was a cue, every swirl of water was a step in this dance of nature.

And as I stood there, feeling the water trickling, sensing the pulse of the city, I realized one thing: we were not just trying to survive a flood; we were in the midst of nature's ballet, where the city danced to a perilous tune. The river had begun its performance, and soon, the sea and the moon would join in.

All I could do was brace myself, calculate, and strategize—to be ready for when the dance would reach its crescendo.

Flooded Floors to Open Doors: A Sanctuary Reclaimed

Chapter - 14

Armored for the Battle

Standing at the hotel's entrance, ready to welcome the imminent onslaught of water, I found myself drifting into a whirlwind of thoughts and strategies, contemplating the moves I needed to make next. But then, something unexpected snapped me out of my reverie, a sudden chill against my feet. Jolted by the sensation, I glanced down to see water creeping up, now an inch deep and seeping into my canvas camouflage shoes.

With an instinctive hand gesture, I called out to Manu, two fingers from my eyes to the water, the classic signal you would see in war movies when a commander is guiding his men to keep a lookout for infiltrators. I sprinted towards the porch and made my way back to my office.

There, always ready and waiting, was a pair of knee-length gumboots in my size, packed and prepared for any such emergency. Today, these boots would be part of my armor.

I have learned from my days in the military hostel that one should never be underdressed for any situation, *'then be it war or a bar.'* Proper attire is not just about appearance; it is about being equipped to tackle any situation head-on. Wearing those boots would give me the mobility I needed to wade through waterlogged areas and lead my team after assessing the threats. After all, it is not just about water, there could be a snake, a live electric wire, or any other hazard lurking beneath, hidden like a booby trap. Being cautious and in proper gear was essential.

Flooded Floors to Open Doors: A Sanctuary Reclaimed

I was back in less than 300 seconds. Roaring like a company commander rallying his troops, I announced to my echelon, *"Aaj koi nai thakega, aaj koi nai rukega, aur jahan padega kam, wahan khada hai hum."* ("Noone will get tired today, no one will fall today, and if anywhere, anyone is less, I will be present there, I will clear the mess") My words reverberated, sending a surge of energy through the team. They knew that this was not just a battle against rising water, but a battle to protect our establishment, our guests, and each other.

The water had climbed a few more inches, and our mere wipers were proving ineffective. I shifted tactics immediately. *"Sandbag bharo aur mujhe do,"* ("Fill the sandbags with sand and give to me") I commanded, ready to fortify our defenses by creating an embankment to prevent water from flooding the stilt parking area. If it managed to reach the elevator wells, it would cripple our efforts to transport necessary items from the basement to the upper floors.

With a sense of urgency, the team sprang into action. Rakesh, our bell boy, grabbed a spade and started filling the sandbags. Soon, every available team member, housekeeping staff, kitchen hands, and front office associates joined in, engaging in various tasks that transcended their usual duties. We formed a human chain, passing sandbags one by one, and built an embankment that diverted the water towards the rainwater sump in the lower basement. The pumps there were working non-stop, discharging water into the main rainwater drain connected to our harvesting tank.

Then, I realized something was not right. I sensed that the water flow was unusual, not consistent with normal rains. Turning to the team, I stated, *"Yeh paani ka flow normal barish jaisa nahi hai, isliye sump mein paani ke intake ko kam karna padega."* *("This waterflow isn't like the flows of normal rains, we have to cut the flow of water to rainwater sumps")* I knew that if we did not control the intake, we risked overwhelming the sump and flooding the basement.

There was a lateral trench near the stilt parking that usually collected water during heavy rains, preventing the area from getting waterlogged. This trench was connected to the main drainage line of the city. Without hesitation, I pulled the grills off the trench and instructed Manu to fit a small 1 HP submersible pump into it. The pump was tiny, but it was the only one that would fit in the narrow space. The pump began to pull water out of the trench and redirected it towards the main drain.

"*Ek aur pump laga do, jo rainwater sump se paani kheench kar directly is tributary pump ke saath mila sake,*" ("Put one more pump which can pull water from rainwater sump and join as a tributary of small pump") I directed, adding another layer of water evacuation to ease the burden on our primary sump. This additional pump would pull water directly from the rainwater sump and release it through the trench, combining forces with the little submersible pump to create a more effective drainage system.

Our makeshift plan was now operational, a network of pumps and trenches working in tandem. As I stood back to observe the setup, I could see the water levels slowly stabilizing, giving us a much-needed breather.

"Manu, keep monitoring the pumps. Ek bhi glitch hua toh, report karo!" ("Manu report if you find any glitches or abnormalities") I barked out orders, knowing that any lapse could turn our temporary victory into a loss. Every pump was crucial, every minute mattered.

The day was not over, but we had managed to hold the line, but only for now. Our plan had bought us time, but time was a fickle ally. We knew the battle was far from over. The waters would rise again, and when they did, we had to be ready.

Taking a deep breath, I looked at my team. Tired but determined, they met my gaze. No one was going to falter. Not today.

Chapter - 15

Fortifying the Stronghold

Flooded Floors to Open Doors: A Sanctuary Reclaimed

Time was slipping by, and I had to make quick decisions. The diesel generator (DG) was working steadily, a beast of a machine that had become our lifeline in the face of power outage. I signaled to Manu to keep an eye on the DG's fuel levels. We needed to ensure that the reservoir was topped up with diesel, and soon we were pouring all the barrels we had left into the reservoir tank. But the real issue was the next refill.

Flooded Floors to Open Doors: A Sanctuary Reclaimed

Mukesh, our timekeeper and security supervisor, approached with a sense of urgency. *"Sir, bahar 4 wheeler se jane mein thoda issue hai, mera scooter hai main leke aata hoon,"* ("Sir there is problem in plying 4-wheeler outside, I have a scooter I can go and fetch the diesel".) he offered, ready to tackle the shortage problem himself. Two-wheelers could easily go throw the narrow strips dodging the water of brimming roads. In his hands, he held two old, dusty canisters. Without missing a beat, I asked him to turn them upside down and show me the contents. As expected, both were completely empty.

Mukesh, unfazed, quickly replied, *"Sir, ab leke jata hoon."* ("Sir, now I will go and get")

"Stop!" I interjected. "Rinse them first with some diesel, it will cleanse all the dirt and rust dwelling inside them. We cannot afford to adulterate the food of this mighty mammoth who is keeping the heart of the hotel alive." My words struck a chord, and Mukesh immediately nodded, heading off with an engineering associate to clean the canisters.

Afterwards they took several rounds, scurrying back and forth, filling all our barrels and the additional canisters with High-Speed Diesel (HSD). Every drop was precious, and I watched as they returned triumphantly, the canisters now full and sloshing with clean fuel. It was a small win, but it felt monumental given the circumstances. At least we had enough reserves to keep the DG running through the night.

Suddenly, my attention was drawn back to the rising water. It was inching closer, creeping up menacingly towards a small opening in the sidewall, the inspection gap for the hotel's CTPT panel. My heart pounded. "Ohh no!" I muttered. The water could easily seep through that gap and reach the DG set from behind. It was like an unguarded border fence, just waiting for infiltrators to sneak through and wreak havoc.

"Get the gravel and cement!" I roared, the urgency in my voice palpable as I grabbed a 5-feet long steel sheet that was lying near the ramp for some repair work. Everyone scattered, knowing the gravity of the situation. Manu and a few others ran to gather the necessary materials, while I placed the steel sheet firmly against the gap in the wall.

Working together in frantic coordination, we began to seal the gap, shoveling gravel and pouring cement over it. A team member from the engineering department slid a piece of tile against the steel sheet from the other side, acting as an extra brace. We layered more cement and gravel until we had a makeshift, but solid, wall of steel and concrete.

As I stood back, covered in dust, and sweat, I surveyed our handiwork. The gap was completely sealed. There was no way the water could sneak in now. I glanced at Mukesh, who was breathing heavily but still had a resolute expression on his face. "Good work," I said. He simply nodded, understanding that there was no time for celebration. The battle was not over yet.

"Sir, aur kuch karna hai kya?" ("Sir is there anything else which needs to be done") Mukesh asked, always ready for the next task.

I paused, looked around, and then turned to him with a slight smile, "For now we have everything covered up, but we have to ensure to keep checking, next time we might not get such luxury of time and resources to solve the problem."

Mukesh nodded firmly, and the team dispersed to reinforce other vulnerable areas. I took a deep breath, feeling the familiar weight of responsibility settle on my shoulders. Every decision, every move, every second was crucial. This was not just about preventing water from flooding the hotel; it was about safeguarding our sanctuary from being overrun by nature's fury.

The DG was protected, for now. But as I looked at the water still rising outside, I knew I could not afford to drop my guard. This war was just beginning, and we needed to be ready for every onslaught nature had in store.

Chapter - 16

A War of Flow and Force

The tug of war had officially begun. The water was gushing in, relentless and unyielding, while our pumps also were struggling to keep up, whirring with the effort of pushing it back out. The only strategy was to overpower the inflow by a few hundred gallons each minute, but every second felt like we were merely delaying the inevitable.

I scanned the premises, eyes darting from one sump to another. The grease trap was bubbling violently, and other sumps were showing similar signs. It was a tell-tale indication that the river's level was rising, causing the drain levels to swell in synchronization. It was like watching a perfect harmony and that too the one that could destroy us if left unchecked.

Running across the basement, I carried yet another heavy sheet of steel towards the vulnerable gap. Each step felt like a battle, the water striking against my gum boots with increasing force. I had seen the wrath of a rising river before, but something about this felt different. The pressure of the water was not just the usual overflow; it was coming with a vengeance. The force was unnaturally strong, as if someone had turned open a sluice gate upstream.

I glanced back at the road leading to Akota. There was no sign of the divider; everything was submerged under the murky brown water. Cars and scooters, once standing on dry ground, were now floating debris, being carried away by the sheer force of the current. The realization hit me like a punch to the gut, this was not just a usual water logging.

Something was fundamentally wrong.

"This can't be the result of rising levels of river," I muttered to myself. With every instinct on high alert, I pulled up my mental database of the past floods, in retrospection I had the way the water had moved, the time it had taken to reach certain areas, and the force it had exerted. But none of it matched or made sense with what I was seeing now. It was as if the river had taken on a life of its own, shifting and surging in ways it never had before.

I felt a chill run down my spine as I looked at the water that was now beginning to swirl in harsh, unpredictable patterns near the entrance. "This is different... there is something severely wrong here or somewhere." My mind raced, trying to piece together this puzzle, but every time I thought I had the answer; the river would behave in a way that defied logic.

I kept replaying the data and past scenarios in my head. The rising levels, the city's drainage capacity, the force of the river's outflow, all of it was supposed to follow a certain rhythm. It was a rhythm I knew well; one I could anticipate and react to. But today, it felt like I had been preparing to face a boar and was instead confronted by a roar of a lion. The attack was different, unexpected, and far more dangerous than anything I had faced before.

I indicated to Manu and the team to double-check the pumps. Every piece of equipment was running at maximum capacity, but the water kept creeping forward, defying our efforts.

"Aur ek pump ka setup ready karo!" ("keep setup of one more pump ready") I shouted, the urgency in my voice resonating through the chaos. We needed more power; more force to combat the rising tide. But deep down, I knew it was not just a matter of mechanics anymore. There was something else, something we could not see and that was shifting the balance against us.

My mind flickered back to the full moon, the tidal pull, the alignment of forces that governed the water's behavior. But even that could not explain this sudden surge. The city's underground drainage system seemed to have turned against us, and the river, our old adversary, was behaving like a stranger, totally unpredictable, wild, and ferocious.

It was as if every element had conspired to push us to the brink.

"Check all the inlets!" I conveyed to the team. "Aur koi bhi galat dikhe, turant mujhe inform karo!" ("Immediately inform me if you find anything wrong or abnormal")

The team nodded and spread-out marching in gumboots, urgency painted across their faces. There was no room for error now. If the water found a way to bypass our defenses, it would mean disaster, not just for the hotel but for everyone inside it.

Taking a deep breath, I looked back at the basement entrance where the water was slowly inching its way. We had been through floods before, but this time, it felt like we were fighting something far more sinister, a force that was playing by its own rules.

And the worst part was, I could not figure out what those rules were.

"This is definitely not just the river," I whispered again to myself, the realization dawning on me with terrifying clarity. "This is something else."

I turned to Mukesh, who was standing beside me, wide-eyed but resolute. *"Mukesh, har team member ko bolo alert rahe. Muster register se saare employees ki list banao, mujhe total employees ki ginti chhaiye, casual ho ya trainee koi nai chootna chaiye,"* ("Mukesh, tell every team member to remain alert. Also make a list of all the employees present in the premises, no name should be left, be it casual intern or industrial intern, list must be perfect") little confused by my statement Mukesh immediately nodded and got into the task.

He hurried off, as if trying to match his urgency to my own. I knew we could not let our guard down, not even for a second. The water was no longer our only enemy. Something else was coming. And whatever it was, it was about to hit us full force.

In the face of uncertainty and fear, I clenched my fists and steeled my resolve. Whatever it took, whatever was coming; we would face it, and we would face it with full force.

The war had escalated, and now it was time to fight like never before.

Chapter - 17

An Unnatural Pattern

I kept revisiting the facts and reconfirming the pattern in my mind. Something was not adding up. I decided to check the building located at the back side of the hotel, which had access from the ramp that led down to the basement floor. This building had been with us for a long time, leased for record-keeping and as the finance office. Originally part of the sprawling Samrajya housing society, this two-story structure also had access from the society's main gate, though we typically used the back gate to access it from our premises.

I took a detour and entered the society through the main gate of the building, not expecting what I saw: the entire society was as dry as a desert. It was utterly baffling. In every flood I had witnessed, the society would be the first to get inundated, followed by water entering through the hotel's entrance. Then, the sumps would swell, and eventually, the basement would start accumulating water. Our strategy in such scenarios was to pump the water out with double the force, ensuring it receded to just a few inches in the basement, where it would remain throughout the flood. This would usually give us a couple of hours of struggle until the water started receding across the city.

But today... today was entirely different.

"What's going on here?" I muttered under my breath, scratching my head in disbelief. The expected sequence of events was not unfolding. There was no sign of water in the society, and yet, the floodwater was already hammering the hotel's entrance.

I tried to decipher the anomaly. *"The society is dry, yet the hotel is getting flooded... That means water is not entering the society at all."* But how was that possible? The society, being at a lower level, should have been the first point of entry for the floodwaters. For the hotel to get inundated like this without society being affected suggested something entirely different was happening.

"Is the water bypassing the society? Is it backflowing from somewhere else?" I pondered. With each moment of analysis, the situation grew more perplexing.

——— - ・ - ———

Chapter - 18

The Deluge Unleashed

I was jolted out of my thoughts by Manu's frantic voice, "Sir... Sirr!!! Basement me paani bharne laga hai!" ("Sir!! The basement is getting waterlogged)

Instantly, I halted the wild horses of my racing mind and sprinted towards the basement using the ramp. What I witnessed confirmed Manu's panic: water had started flooding the basement, surging in with an alarming intensity, and the entrance of the hotel had turned into a conduit for the water, making the roads outside look like a riverbed. The flow had outmatched us; it was overpowering us by hundreds of gallons every few seconds.

We needed a bigger pump. But merely arranging one was not going to solve the problem. A high-capacity pump required a three-phase motor and a starter, along with a three-phase connection setup. Moreover, the foot valve of such pumps is typically larger and requires deeper water to function effectively. Gathering the equipment, setting it up, and securing the necessary connections would eat up time, a luxury we could not afford. And for it to work, because of a bigger foot valve I would need deeper water in my basement. Ironically, that was the last thing I ever wanted.

My mind spun like a turbo engine, racing to figure out a solution. I abruptly shouted, "Manu! Saare sumps ka dhakkan thoda thoda khol do!" ("Manu open the lids of all the sumps a bit")

Manu looked bewildered for a second, but responded quickly, "Sirrr... ohhkk... accha sir!"

I rushed towards the drain sumps located in the basement and opened all three chambers slightly, just enough for the water to flow inside but still covered enough so that no one would accidentally step in and get hurt. This quick decision-making stemmed from my hands-on experience with the engineering team during major preventive maintenance checks and repairs. Those moments had ingrained in me the technical expertise that was now proving invaluable.

In one of the sumps, we had a powerful submersible cutter pump installed, capable of even grinding small stones while draining water. I turned it on, and water started flowing into the main sumps and receding. But I knew this was only a temporary relief; the source of the water surge needed to be addressed.

Turning my focus back to the team, I shouted out instructions. "Chef, take out whatever necessary items you have from the basement. And listen carefully—*koi basement me akela nai rahega, koi matlab koi bhi. Paani hai chahe nai hai, agar do aadmi kaam kar rahe hai aur dusre ko toilet jana ho, to bhi dono ek saath bahar niklenge. Is that understood?*" ("Nobody would stay in the basement alone, nobody means NOBODY, irrespective now whether there is water logging or not, if two persons are working and one has to go to answer nature's call, then also both has to vacate the premises together").

Chef, clearly rattled by the unusual command, nodded fervently, and replied in a single breath, *"Ji sir, bilkul sir!"* *("yes sir, absolutely sir")*

The basement's water levels were gradually receding, but with every inch of water going down, my anxiety was climbing higher. Something was terribly wrong.

"Something is wrong... something is wrong," I could not stop murmuring like a fanatic chant under my every breath, unable to shake the nagging feeling that a storm, much greater than what I could anticipate, was about to descend upon us.

Chapter - 19

The Missing Piece

Dwelling deep in my thought, I called out to Manu, *"Manu, basement aur pump ka dhyan rakho, main abhi aata hoon."* ("Manu, take care of the pumps and basement, I will just be back") I needed the missing piece of information, something like a crucial formula or fraction required to complete a theorem. Something was not adding up. The water flow, the pattern, the intensity, it all felt irregular, and I had to find out why.

I climbed up to the terrace and glanced at the society just behind the hotel. The sight sent shivers to my mind. The society was still completely dry. This was not making any sense; it needed more scrutiny. My instincts told me that something catastrophic was unfolding behind the scenes.

Driven by urgency, I climbed further up, past the overhead water storage, and made my way to the highest point of the building where our solar heating panels were installed. The sight that greeted me made my heart pound furiously in my chest, the retention wall of the river, just before this part of the society, was shattered and was crumbling away piece by piece.

"OHH MY GOD!!!" I exclaimed aloud.

The realization hit me like a lightning bolt: this time, water would not seep in slowly from the back or the sides. *This time!* it would face us head-on, coming down the road with ferocious force, turning the street into a raging river. The water would pummel through the entrance with unrelenting power, as if the river itself were setting out to reclaim the land we were desperately trying to hold onto.

All our efforts, everything we had been doing, would buy us only a few hours at most. And that is if we were lucky.

I could now only hope that those few hours would coincide with the peak of the flood, and that by some miracle, the water would recede soon afterward.

Calming myself, I descended back to the entrance. The water level was visibly rising. The pipes meant to expel water outside were now bobbing and turning back towards the hotel, like snakes whipped by the current.

"Sir, baar baar theek kar raha hoon, phir bhi wapas mud raha hai pipe!" Mukesh exclaimed in exasperation. ("Sir I am mending it again and again but its bending back")

"Rehne do, aur motor bhi band kar do. Iske force se jyada paani ka force hai. Sirf basement wala chalne do," ("Just leave it and switch off the motor too, water currents have more force inwards. Only let the basement pumps be functional") I replied, acknowledging Mukesh's efforts and telling him to ease off.

I had to remain absolutely calm and think with utmost clarity. Any wrong move made in panic could spell disaster in a split second, turning the controlled chaos against us into a single blow. I rushed to the basement, where our strategy of pushing water out was slowly being thwarted. The mini puddles that had been forming were now turning into small pools.

I turned to the FBM, who was supervising the relocation of crockery and linen from his store. *"Remove this ice cube machine as well, else it will get damaged even with shallow water!"*

Without hesitation, everyone got to work on that task. The clock was ticking, and my mind raced, analyzing every outcome, and contemplating every move we could make.

It was now clear: flooding was inevitable. The only questions left were when it would happen and to what extent the damage would go.

Flooded Floors to Open Doors: A Sanctuary Reclaimed

Chapter - 20

The Rising Tide

Water on the road just outside the hotel started to surge back and forth, and the relentless gushing began to flood into the hotel premises. It was clear now: the hotel was under the imminent threat of floodwater, influenced by multiple uncontrollable factors. As the water level continued to rise, I called Manu to check on the service elevators, instructing him to take both elevators on the top floor offline before the rising water in the stilt parking breached the tile barricades, we had put up at the elevator doors. Manu quickly went up and took care of it.

When he returned, I announced that no further evacuations would be conducted and instructed him to cut the power to the basement floor. As I glanced toward the two cars parked inside, I was about to call someone for an update when I heard a voice.

"I think I should get my car on the ramp of the hotel's porch," said a guest who had shifted to the hotel because his house was inundated. An ex-Air Force veteran, he exuded worry and experience. We quickly facilitated that move. While maneuvering the car out, I noticed the water was already ankle-deep in the parking area.

"Everyone, vacate the area and head up to the building!" I called out. I also told Mukesh to fetch me a list of all the employees. But before he could get the list, I suddenly snapped, *"Oh, where is the chef? I have not seen him in a while!"* A thought struck me, and I leaped into the water, making my way toward the basement with calculated, brisk steps. The water was rushing in like a fierce current.

As I reached the basement, the water was already above my ankles, and at the rate it was filling, it would soon surpass safe levels. I pulled out the flashlight we had kept at the front office, housekeeping, and engineering for emergencies. To my horror, I saw Chef and his team hauling goods from the basement up the stairs, with Chef barking orders at someone in the farthest corner while moving ahead.

"Chef, ye kya chal raha hai? Maine mana kiya tha basement mein jaane ko! Aur peeche kisko chhod aaye ho wahan akela?" I shouted. ("Chef, what all is happening here, I have told to not go to the basement, and who have you left you behind on that corner")

The chef grinned sheepishly again. *"Sir, thoda breakfast aur dinner ka samaan lene aaya hoon,"* he replied innocently. ("Sir just got to get some stuff for breakfast and dinner")

I was completely aghast. Keeping my composure, I said, *"Aur maine mana kiya tha basement mein kisi ko akela nahi chhodna hai, kuch bhi ho jaaye. Bulao usko abhi ke abhi!"* ("And I had clearly told that no one to be left alone or behind in the basement come what may, call that person back right now") I shouted, moving toward the far end of the basement. I announced furiously that the basement was now *"out of bounds"* for everyone.

"Bahar niklo yahan se! Jo samaan upar rakhwaya hai, usse manage kar lenge lekin ab aur koi basement mein nahi aayega!" *("Everyone get out of here, whatever stuff we have kept up stores we will manage from that, nobody should be seen lurking in basement anymore").* I was, although at one thought, appreciative of the chef's commitment towards the guests as well as his conviction to serve the best quality and variety of food to guests as well as the staff, but the kind of risk was not at all worth.

After ensuring everyone had vacated the basement, I hurried back up the ramp. Looking back, I noticed the hollowware and other items starting to float as the water level breached safety limits in mere seconds.

I rushed to the FOM and insisted that a headcount to be done immediately to ensure every person who had reported was included and their location identified. I instructed everyone to check for their colleagues, calling out to identify those who were missing. I was reiterating the same sentences over and over, my mind racing with anxiety as I thought about the potential disaster unfolding. Recently, we had heard about IAS aspirants who drowned in a basement during a flood in Delhi.

Basements are perilous when floodwaters invade. People often think they can enter and exit quickly, but that is rarely the case.

1. **Basements fill up quickly**, transforming a ten-feet high space into a water body in mere minutes.

2. **Entry of water and exit of person are often the same route**; in most cases, this traps a person within the rising waters before they can escape.

The thought of an averted disaster ignited a surge of adrenaline within me. I clenched my jaw and murmured to myself, *"I may lose a lot today, but I am not losing a single man—not here, not under my watch."*

Chapter - 21

Rising Challenges, Deepening Waters

I quickly called Manu. *"Manu, ab pani aur badh raha hai. Guest elevator band karna padega. Jab main bolun, turant elevator upar leke band kar dena."* ("Manu the water levels are rising, we will have to shut down the guest elevators, the moment I say, take the elevator cars up floor and shut them down")

Then I called the FOM and asked him to inform all guests that we would be shutting down the elevators in a few minutes. Once I confirmed that everyone was notified about it, I gave Manu the signal to shut down the guest elevators.

The basement was filling up at an alarming rate, and my concern turned to the Water Treatment Plant (WTP) motors. The WTP was in an adjacent basement connected only through a drain line that we had already sealed to prevent flooding. But how long would it hold? Once the main basement filled up, water would start spreading and could flood the adjacent basement via the stairs, filling it from the top instead of the bottom.

I immediately instructed Manu, "Run the motors on manual and fill the OHT (Overhead Tank) to the brim. Keep doing this until water starts entering the admin basement or until we need to cut the power."

I went back to the hotel entrance, where the water level had risen a few more inches. There was still one more car left in the stilt parking, but there was no place to move it. The hotel's ramp was already full of cars parked in three rows. I looked around and saw that there was no scope of taking the car outside the premises.

Thinking on my feet, I instructed, "Park one of the cars on the declining ramp of the exit gate, right in the middle." Once I saw that the car could be accommodated there, I took a deep breath. This was precisely why I never brought my own car to the hotel; I did not want to worry about anything personal. I wanted all my attention to be focused on the hotel and everything related to it.

I called the valet for the keys and instructed him to get the car. Just then, the guest who owned the car arrived. Coincidentally, he was also an Air Force officer on his way to Bhuj and had gotten stuck here during transit.

"Arey, baaki sab ki car upar hai, bas meri car yahan par hai. Ab kya hoga, ye toh khatam hai ab bass," ("Everybody's car is held up, only mine is left here, what will happen now, the car is finished for sure") he said in dismay.

I quickly held him and reassured him, "Do not come into the water. I am on it; we will get your car safely to the ramp." I instructed the valet not to press the accelerator too hard, and I decided to push the car myself. Watching this, more team members joined in, and together, we pushed the car up to the ramp until it was safe.

Time passed, and now the basement was completely submerged under floodwater. The stationary and dry stores, walk-in fridges, entire bakery, prep kitchen, softener plant, admin office, GM's office, F&B linen store—everything was consumed by the relentless floodwaters. But despite everything, the hotel stood erect, defying the flood's might.

I did not show even a hint of disappointment to anyone. I congratulated everyone for their hard work and told them, *"Let's focus on making maximum efforts to ensure our guests are comfortable and not panicking."*

Just then, I got a call from my wife. After exchanging pleasantries and checking on each other's well-being, we talked about some casual things. She then shared excitedly, *"Did you see the 'Our Vadodara' handle? They are showing so much water everywhere! What is the situation there? Paani aaya kya?"*

I hesitated before replying. "Yes, the roads are flooded and so is the Vishwamitri River," I said, trying to keep my voice steady. I did not want her to sense the enormity of the situation with which I was dealing.

"Photos bhejo na! I wish to see!" she said nonchalantly.

I could not respond to her request immediately. I just smiled and said, *"Dekhta hoon." ("Will see if I could")*

The day was at its peak, and so was the flood.

Chapter - 22

Shutting Down the Heartbeat

I stood on the ramp of the hotel's porch, watching the murky water rise steadily, inch by inch. My mind was racing, continuously thinking about what more could have been done but more importantly what must be done next. I had already instructed the FOM to inform all the guests about being careful while using water, as the clean, usable water we had in storage was our only reservoir left amidst this sea of filth surrounding us.

Most hotels, like ours, have a two-button flushing system—one for a half flush and the other for a full flush. In times of water scarcity, it is advisable to use the half flush:

1. It helps conserve water.
2. In case the water supply to the line, or overhead tank, depletes completely; you would still have one more attempt left to flush.

Water rose increasingly; I was paying close attention to every inch it crept upwards. At this moment of distress, every second of ease was essential. I kept my gaze fixed on a particular point, praying silently that the water would not reach that critical mark.

But as fate would have it, the inevitable finally happened, the filthy water reached that dreaded point. My heart sank as I signaled Manu, "Manu, the time is up. Kill the power."

We had already informed our guests that if the water level rose beyond a certain point, we would have to shut down the DG set (Diesel Generator), as water entering the DG's alternator would cause irreparable damage.

Manu immediately pushed the manual button to shut down the DG, and with a wheezing whir and a final thud, the hotel's lifeline, its power source, came to a halt. I walked over to the AMF (Automatic Mains Failure) panel, pushed the breaker to stop, and regulated the supply to "off" from both the DG and the raw power. From this point onward, I wanted the power to be turned back on only with my permission, only after I had verified that the water was not compromising any electrical panels, and only if it was absolutely safe to do so.

Although I knew that getting raw power from the grid at this point was out of the question, but this was me, *keeping the hope alive while practicing utmost caution.*

An unsettling silence enveloped the entire premises. The only sound was that of the water gushing and swirling around in various corners. The usual humming of the machinery, the comforting buzz of lights, and the consistent thrum of the DG were all replaced by an eerie quietness that highlighted our vulnerability in the face of nature's fury.

It felt as though the hotel itself had taken a deep breath and paused, preparing to endure what was yet to come.

Chapter - 23

The Weight of the Sky

Standing at the main porch, I looked up at the sky, taking a deep breath as I tried to read the weather like an ancient mariner scanning the horizon for hope. The clouds were dense, black in one direction, and still blue in patches elsewhere, but the sun was retreating behind them, like it was ashamed that the day had gone so wrong. Below, the city was drowning, and the roads that were once pathways of movement were now rivers of stillness. The world seemed to slow down, submerged under the water and weight of sky and uncertainty.

I pulled out my phone and began calling other hotel GMs. *Someone may have any idea. Someone had avoided the worst. If needed, I could find a safe place to relocate my guests.* But with every call, I received the same grim response, each one struggling as I was.

Floodwaters did not discriminate between status, stars, or plans. "Please take care of your people," I told each one. It was the only advice that seemed to matter now. Staff, guests, they were all in the same fragile boat.

The empty streets from earlier had transformed into something resembling a riverbank. Cars, once carefully parked along the sides, were now half-submerged, their owners no doubt hoped that the water would not climb any higher. But it did. The water on the ramps leading to the porch surged and receded like tidal waves, lapping closer and closer to the building, testing its defenses.

I looked around and calculated, almost 70 guests, including children and the elderly, and 40 plus staff members. All of them were my responsibility. I ran a mental scenario: *If this flood follows the usual pattern, it should start receding by evening. But if the city has absorbed more water than expected, then it could take even the night, maybe the morning tomorrow will be glittery.* A hazy glimmer of hope flickered in my mind, but it was laced with uncertainty.

On the porch, guests had started to gather, watching the flood unfold like a grim spectacle of nature. Each face held a different expression, some were excited by the rarity of the moment, others were anxious, disappointed, jittery, angry. It was a kaleidoscope of human emotions standing in front of me, a collage of uncertainty and expectation.

Dressed in my camo greens, visibly the in-charge, I quickly became the target of a flood of questions, each one like the rushing water, piling on top of me. Their voices overlapped, concerned, and confused, desperate for some assurance. I knew I had to address them, not just to explain the situation but to manage their fear. I spoke calmly, walking them through the situation, the city's geography, the way the river swells in the monsoon, how the rain behaves, and why the hotel was positioned the way it was.

But I did not just stick to dry facts. I kept things light, adding in the occasional joke, throwing in a few amusing anecdotes, and even rhyming a little when I could. I had to give them something more than information; I had to give them hope. People do not just need to hear what is happening during a crisis; they need to *feel* that someone is in control, that someone knows what they are doing. If I could make them smile, even laugh, for a moment, it would help them feel calmer, safer.

In moments of chaos, mass confidence is as important as mass cooperation. The group needs to move as one, listen as one, and trust the voice guiding them. Otherwise, the real danger is not just the flood outside, it is the panic that can break out inside. That is what I had to prevent. As I spoke, I could feel the tension ease, just a little. The questions slowed down, and I saw a few guests nodding, their shoulders relaxing. They believed in me, and that was half the battle won.

Flooded Floors to Open Doors: A Sanctuary Reclaimed

Chapter - 24

The Art of Survival

The day dragged on with the same stubborn persistence as the floodwaters, refusing to offer even an inch of hope that the worst was behind us. I had clung to the belief that perhaps by evening, the water would begin to recede, that nature might offer a silent truce as the sun would set. Even in the mighty war of *Mahabharata,* the sunset would bring immediate truce irrespective of the level of escalation in war. But nature does not follow the predictable order of human expectation, it has no obligation to grant us mercy or any mundane protocols to adhere to. The evening came without a hint of respite, leaving us to face another night of uncertainty.

Sunset was near and surrender was not an option. We had to adapt, improvise, and push through. Gathering the team around me, I could see the strain in their faces, the weariness of the day etched into every expression. But beneath that, I could also see determination. "We need to conserve as much water and food as possible," I said, my voice steady. "No more elaborate buffets, but the meals still need to be satisfying. We need to make sure the guests do not feel like they are trapped, they should feel like they are camping. It is all about perception."

Perception is a tricky thing, I reflected. The situation could feel like either a catastrophe or an adventure, depending on how we framed it. Our job now was to create an impression of calm control, even when the reality was far from it.

I turned to the chef. "We will start preparing dinner before sunset. We do not have power, so we need to save what emergency lighting we have. And no wasting of water on cleaning up other areas apart from food and stations, cuisine hygiene is important; used utensils should be wiped down and stacked away. We will use disposable plates and cutlery if necessary. Garbage needs to be minimized and sealed tightly in bags, leave them a quarter empty so they can be securely tied off."

Although the situation outside did not offer much comfort; the word had come that there was still a small dry patch near Shivaji Circle, where a few general and medical stores were open, untouched by the rising water. I quickly formed a team of four and equipped them with large sticks to rake the water ahead as they walked. Their task was to ensure the path was free of potholes or obstructions, as they waded through knee-deep water to retrieve supplies. I gave them a list of essentials: deodorants (since bathing would not be an option for long), medicines, and bulk candles to light up the night ahead.

The survival training I had undergone in the past was coming back to me now, the lessons in crisis management and first aid paying off. I instructed the team to retrieve a variety of medicines: antipyretics, analgesics, antiemetics, and even emergency medicines like sorbitrate. We needed to be prepared for everything.

Returning to the lobby, I addressed the team again. "The EPBAX system is still running on the UPS, so telecom is active. Make sure to attend to all guest needs with absolute courtesy and care. And remember, as there is no power and elevators are not functional, we will handle room service for elderly guests or those with special needs only. Focus on making our guests feel comfortable and safe."

The FOM approached me, asking whether I would like to move to a lower floor for convenience. I smiled and shook my head. "No, my room has the perfect view of the river. I need to keep an eye on the water's rise. I can jump, crawl, creep, or climb to get back there if I must, but I am not leaving my post." Please shift elderly people and people with preferences to the lower floors.

I clapped my hands to get everyone's attention. "Listen up," I said. "This experience is not in any of our training manuals, but it is going to be now. Take this as a live drill, an opportunity to learn and grow. We are in this together, and we will come out of it stronger. Now, let us focus on our guests and give them a great candlelight dinner tonight."

With those words, the team scattered to their tasks, and I stood at the porch, watching as the waters rose ever so slowly. The day might not have ended with a resolution, but we were still in control. Or at least, we needed to make it seem that way.

Chapter - 25

Candlelight and Crisis

The restaurant buzzed with the soft clatter of cutlery on crockery, as guests joyfully enjoyed their meal under the gleam of candlelight. No streaming music, no fancy lighting, no LED displays, yet the atmosphere was warm and celebratory. It felt like a scene from a Hollywood's history period film, where villagers gathered for a communal feast, their faces glowing with the flickering light, and the air filled with laughter and conversation. ***A happy dwelling hamlet.***

I moved through the restaurant, quietly observing the scene, and approached the FBM to inquire about the feedback on the meal. *Were the guests satisfied? Did the elderly receive their meals without trouble?* The answer was a resounding *yes*. Despite the situation, people were in good spirits, and that was a relief. The perception of normalcy, however fragile, was holding on.

Next, I made my way to the hall where the staff were having their meal. A quick chat here, a few pep talk there, it was all about boosting morale. The team had been working non-stop, and they needed to feel appreciated. I personally relieved the engineering crew, who had been at my side the entire day, and sent them off for a much-deserved meal break. Meanwhile, I settled in the lobby, my eyes scanning the faces of everyone I saw, reading their body language through the hazy light of the flickering candles. Everyone was calm, for now.

One of the elderly guests approached me with a concern: her phone was dying, and she had no way to charge it. I did not hesitate. I immediately instructed the FOM to bring one of the UPS units from the office to charge her phone. At the same time, I reminded him to charge his own phone from the second port of the UPS. Communication devices were critical in this situation. Without them, we would get cut off from the outside world, so I quickly issued new instructions to the team, disable Bluetooth, Wi-Fi, and mobile data to conserve battery life.

All phones were to be set to power-saving mode.

The most important phones, the ones belonging to staff and key personnel, were charged using the remaining UPS units, which had been salvaged from the admin office. I knew that by doing this, we would have enough power to keep our devices functional for the night and hopefully a few hours into the morning. Most of the phones were drained, but we were hopeful that the worst of the flood would pass soon. In the morning, communication lines would reopen, and help could reach us.

In times of crisis, every resource counts, and how we use those resources can be the difference between order and chaos. It was not just about having enough supplies; it was about knowing what to prioritize, when to act, and how to make decisions that would mitigate as many uncertainties as possible.

Standing in the dim, candlelit lobby, I could see the trust that had been built, between the guests and the staff, between each team member. And as I watched the shadows flicker on the walls, I realized that in moments like this, survival was not just about the physical. It was about maintaining hope, control, and the delicate balance of the human spirit.

Chapter - 26

Cooling the Heat of Crisis

The night had fallen, and for a brief moment, it felt the day was won. I was silently celebrating, thinking, *"A Day saved."* But just as I was beginning to feel triumphant, my phone rang. It was the FOM, sounding perplexed and worried.

"Sir, a few guests are complaining that their rooms are warm. What should we do? Should I have the windows opened?"

I immediately understood the dilemma. Though the weather outside was pleasant, the combination of latent heat and body warmth in an enclosed space could easily make a room feel stifling. Opening the windows seemed like the simplest solution, but was it the safest?

"No," I replied without hesitation. Opening windows in high-rise buildings without protective grills was a serious safety concern. And provided the scenario of floods there was also the risk of inviting insects, mosquitoes, that maggot carrying flesh flies, wasps, gnats, bees and even bats from the dense flora lining the banks of the Viswamitri river. This was not just an inconvenience; it could be a safety issue for our guests. But what was the alternative?

I could not simply tell them that nothing could be done. We had to offer a solution, even if it was just a placebo or something more creative.

My mind raced. How could we cool the rooms without air conditioning? And then, suddenly, an idea struck me. Air conditioner's function is based on heat exchange, what if we could use the chilly weather outside for a natural heat exchange?

I quickly instructed the FOM, "Tell the guests to fully open both their heavy and sheer curtains. This will expose the cooler walls of the room to the inside air, as curtains not only act as insulation from light but also the temperature and differential temperature can be used in case weather is cooler outside, and over time, the whole room should cool down."

It was a simple but effective idea. Within half an hour, the results were noticeable. The rooms began to feel cooler, and we rolled out the suggestion to the rest of the guests. Some might not have complained but were feeling and enduring discomfort silently. This small trick could help them too. It was a win, a small but important victory in maintaining comfort in the face of adversity.

As the night deepened, I felt a wave of exhaustion hit me. The day had been relentless, and I had barely stopped to catch my breath. That is when the Chef approached me with a hopeful look on his face.

"Aapke liye ye sab bana deta hoon," ("Sir, let me prepare all this for you") he said, presenting a list of an elaborate five-course meal. Everyone knew that I was quite particular about my food, small, balanced meals, just enough to keep going. I often joked, *"I only eat to survive,"* and my meals, when I dined alone, were known to last no more than five minutes, from serving to clearing the plates.

The chef was clearly trying to treat his commander after the long day, as a gesture of gratitude for steering the team and keeping everyone safe. But I was not in the mood for a grand feast.

"Nahi, Chef," I smiled. *"Thoda khichdi khaunga bas."* ("I will have some Khichdi only")

"Sir, kuch to special le lo aaj," ("Sir, have something special today at least") he pressed gently, wanting to offer something extra.

"Theek hai, fir thoda achar de dena," ("Alright, give me some pickle") I relented, grinning. It had been years since I had tasted pickle, and the Chef understood it was special in its own way.

The gesture reminded me of the small joys that can arise during chaos. As I sat down, I realized that sometimes, it is the quiet, thoughtful, and calm moments that help anchor us during a storm.

Chapter – 27

The Weight of Darkness

The kitchen was closing, and it was already too late. I picked up my food packet, my habitual last meal of the day always reserved for after offering a prayer, an acknowledgment to the Almighty for the strength, courage, and resources He bestowed upon me to carry out this challenging role. Life was beautiful, even in chaos. I often thanked the divine for the opportunity to stand at the helm, steering through storms. Being grateful is motivational too, we often forget about the achievements we acquire on daily basis and keep on complaining about the aspirations we haven't even have the cognizance of, we don't even know how exactly we will feel when the aspiration comes true, and constantly lurking for the untasted palate we choose to ignore the very palpable experiences. For example, *being able to get a dining experience which would be a surprise to our taste buds, as well, is a moment of gratitude.*

Climbing to my room on the top floor, I used the faint light of my mobile screen. Battery preservation was key, and after countless trips up and down those stairs, the path was etched into my bones. My steps were slow, measured, like a metronome that had already marked the tempo of survival.

When I finally reached my room and freshened up, the gentle hiss of the half-flush filling the tank caught my attention. I knew without needing to check, that water would last only until morning. Survival instincts kicked in, learned from old lessons, and honed through experience. I filled two bottles: one for a makeshift drip shower and one for emergencies. It is remarkable how long a single Liter of water can stretch, how it can become a day's worth of necessity in the hands of someone who knows.

I sat on the sofa, offering a silent prayer. Gratitude flowed for the unseen strength that held me upright amidst the storm, and for the life that, despite the flood, was still brimming with wonder. Then came the simple delight of opening the food packet, a humble box of khichdi, comforting like a warm embrace after a drawn-out battle.

The day had worn me down. My feet throbbed, encased for hours in those knee-length gum boots, each weighing more than a kilo. As I massaged my tired legs, a soft vibration from my smart watch drew my attention, it was congratulating me. "Most Active Day," it said, with a step count of 40,000+ and 90 floors climbed. "Seems like it's in a hurry to award me a gallantry medal before the war is even won," I chuckled to myself, amused by the irony.

It was midnight, and the watch's battery was just as exhausted as I was. I checked my phone, scanning for updates on the river and dam levels. The data was disheartening; the Ajwa Dam was still at 213.72 feet, and the river showed no sign of calming down. I pulled open the curtains for a firsthand look at the Viswamitri, which lay beneath the twilight, still swollen and defiant.

The city had surrendered to darkness. Not a single building illuminated, no signs, no lights, only the melancholics blinking of submerged car dashboards, their warning signals flickering like desperate cries for help. The silence was louder than any siren. Below, now Samrajya society also had succumbed to the encroaching waters, a fortress now taken over by the tide. It felt like the entire city was holding its breath, bracing for the next wave.

Leaving the curtains open, I lay on my bed. Tomorrow would be another battle or respite, a new chapter of challenges and unknown tests or a day of happiness and rejoice, my mind kept on playing the scenarios in oxymoron. I had to be ready. There was so much at stake, so many eyes looking to me for answers, for leadership. I would have to innovate, to find solutions in the chaos, to hope for the best but at the same time ready for the worst.

"A leader never falls, a leader never fails," I kept repeating to myself, like a marine on a mission, steadfast even when the world seemed ready to crumble around me. *Failure does not mean that the task in mind was not achieved, failure is when you succumb to defeat and give up all the feat, if someone silently or violently, irrespectively just gives up; and then that is the fall that is the failure.* Among the revered chant chase through this the fatigue of the day slowly won over, and before I knew it: Sleep! though not the deepest but washed over me, like the temporary calm before the next storm.

Chapter - 28

The Morning Without Respite

As the first rays of light pierced through the window, I jolted awoke and sprang from my bed, racing to the window to get a glimpse of the river. I had hoped, prayed even, that the morning would bring some relief, a change much required and dearly awaited, a shift in the tide. But there was no respite. The river was still bloated and angry, and the sky offered no solace. I had thought the dawn would be different, that the night would have somehow softened the flood's grip. But this time, the water, the weather, and the river had conspired to rewrite the script, to change the very course of what we had come to expect.

The morning, which was meant to be a beacon of hope, seemed to mock us instead.

I rushed to the washroom, ready to tackle the day, only to be met with the hollow silence of a half empty flush tank, but the trick worked now, and the other half flush tank was handy. Being on the top floor meant my water had already run out. I could imagine the pipes below still holding the last few precious liters for those on the lower floors, but for me, the taps were dry. The half liter of water I had wisely set aside last night proved invaluable. It was just enough for my morning routine, a drip here, a splash there. Survival, at its core.

Pulling another camo-green t-shirt from my bag and slipping into a fresh pair of socks, I donned my trusty gum boots, ready for another day of battle. As I descended the stairs, taking in the faint scent of damp walls and the quiet tumult of activity, I was being prepared for the day's new challenges.

But downstairs, a new problem had already started brewing. Scarcity was rearing its head, not just for wash water, but for drinking water and cooking as well. With a household of over 100 people, water consumption was high, especially since mostly everyone was cooped up inside since the evening before yesterday. Just drinking water alone required per day was about 350 to 400 liters. And this was only day 2, meant another hundreds of liters of water.

We still had some RO water stored in a separate tank at the top, but it would not last long if we were not careful. I needed every drop to be used wisely, especially since the staff was working hard without air conditioning or fans, which only made them thirstier.

I called Chef immediately. "*Khane me koi bhi type ke mirchi, pepper ya garam masala nai dalega, na guest ke khane me na staff ke khane me. Jitna ho sake fried items bhi avoid karo.*" ("Food has to be prepared without chillies, peppers or hot spices, for both guests as well as staff, also avoid the deep-fried items where we can")

Spicy and fried foods would only make people thirstier, increase their body heat, and potentially make them irritable, it would prove to be a '*recipe for unrest*' in a situation already fraught with tension. I needed everyone calm, focused, and, most importantly, hydrated. It would also lessen the need for air conditioning, something which was not achievable at this time as power resumption would be the last thing which will happen after such catastrophic inundation.

Next, I called the housekeeping supervisor. "Please inform all guests that we will clean their rooms, but we will not be able to do water-based cleaning or process laundry. We will replace the necessary linens from our par stock. The guests who require flushing their WC, provide them with buckets full of water from the stream outside, the flowing water is muddy but can be used for flushing. Also, give each room extra toilet rolls, we have plenty in supply."

As time passed, guests started gathering for breakfast. To my relief, they not only seemed content, rather enjoying the light, *saatwik* breakfast of non-spicy food items. Faces gleamed with contentment, and many offered me respectful nods or grateful eye gestures. Their trust and calm demeaners maybe were small victories, but victories, nonetheless.

Leaving the restaurant, I went to check on the staff. They too looked worn, but their spirits were adorned. Their united *'namaste'* was a silent reassurance, they were ready for whatever comes next.

After a few critical instructions to the engineering team, I walked up to the porch, only to be greeted by Mr. Mitesh, a guest who had grown fond of our resilience.

"*Are GM Saab, aap toh bahut chamak rahe ho!*" ("Hey! GM Sir, you look absolutely shining") he said with enthusiasm.

"*Aapko pata hai GM sir 1 bottle pani se poora naha dho ke fresh bhi ho jaate hai,*" ("Do you know GM sir get freshen up and bathe by using just one bottle of water") chimed in the bell boy, beaming with pride.

"*Mujhe toh chamakna hi padega, baadal bahut gehre chaaye hain,*" ("I have to and ought to shine as the clouds are pretty dark") I replied with a subtle smile, trying to keep the tone light despite the weight of the day.

Mr. Mitesh and a few others joined in, praising our efforts, acknowledging the teamwork, the planning, and the relentless battle we were all fighting. Their faith in me, in my team, in our ability to carry them through this, was a powerful force. It fueled me, strengthened me and in turn the entire team.

The day had only just begun, but I was ready. Ready for the fight, for the unknown challenges that were bound to surface. Whatever came next, I knew I had the resolve to face it. With their trust behind me and a mind focused on solutions, I felt the power of leadership surge through me.

Irrespective of anything, we would prevail.

Chapter - 29

Tapping the Skies

The lowest tap finally oozed out its last drop, and with that, the entire line fell silent. Dry. Depleted. It was a stark, ominous silence, as if the very pipes themselves were gasping for breath.

"*We will need water to cook food and to serve to guests at least,*" the chef's voice cracked with desperation. His usual confidence was beginning to waver, and I could see the stress pulling at the edges of his expression.

"I'm aware," I responded, trying to project a calm I did not entirely feel. "I've been thinking through solutions." Breakfast had just wrapped up, and while lunch seemed to look like an insurmountable obstacle, I was not just concerned about the next meal. I needed a plan that would carry us through till tomorrow morning. That meant water to drink, water to cook, and some to clean, if at all we were lucky.

"*Let's hope today will be a little better,*" I said, trying to inject a sense of hope into the room. But before the words even settled in the air, they were shattered by one of the team members shouting, "*Sir, lag nai raha hai! Ye dekho, firse baarish aayi hai zor se!*" ("Sir, it doesn't seem so, see its pouring again heavily")

The rain had returned, more ferocious than before. Torrents came pouring down, as if the sky had finally decided to empty its reserves on us. The bell boy, exasperated, threw up his hands, "*Ab aur kitna paani barsega!*" ("Now, how much water will it still pour")

"Paani!" It surrounded us, thousands of cubic feet of it, ironically! but none of it was what we needed. We did not need the murky and muddy floodwaters that had risen menacingly around us. We needed something clean, clear, and usable. Was it ironic! No! cruel, that we were drowning in water, yet thirsting for it at the same time.

Then, like a bolt of lightning, the idea struck. My mind raced ahead of the moment, seizing the opportunity the storm had presented. I turned to the Chef and the F&B Manager, "*Take all the clean utensils you have, and get them up to the terrace. When our taps are dry, we will use the taps pouring from above!*" I pointed towards the clouds, and in an instant, my team sprang into action. It was as if a war had broken out, with dozens of staff members charging towards the terrace, carrying every utensil, bowl, tray, and pot they could lay their hands on. The terrace became a battlefield of hope, the rain our only ally. We were harvesting the storm.

It is remarkable how necessity can shift perceptions. Just moments ago, the rain had been our enemy, an unrelenting force pushing us further into chaos. Now, it was our salvation. We were praying for the very thing we had dreaded, hoping the downpour would continue long enough to meet our needs.

But fate, as always, had its own sense of irony. The moment it saw us turning its weapon into a shield, the clouds relented. The rain began to taper off, teasing us with just enough water to fill our pots and pans, but not enough to rest easily.

Still, it was a victory. "*Water for lunch is arranged,*" I declared, feeling the collective sigh of relief ripple through the team. But as quickly as the relief came, another problem surfaced.

"*Sir, there is no water left for drinking, and the tap of the RO tank is also dry,*" reported the housekeeping supervisor, his face strained and tired.

"*Manu,*" I turned to the engineering supervisor, "*arrange to provide one liter of drinking water per guest. Politely urge them that we shall provide more if needed, but for now, this is what we have.*" I added a wink, and a small grin crept onto my face. I had kept the main valve of RO water tank shut, to avoid any misuse, or accidental pilferage, water of life was necessary and so was to safeguard it.

The team, momentarily stunned, broke into smiles. "*Boss always has a trump card with him,*" one of them murmured, and the mood lifted. "*Issue water to the employees as well,*" I said, finishing the command. The immediate crisis was quelled. We had water, enough to get through lunch and provide at least a ration of drinking water to everyone.

But I could not relax. I was thinking far beyond the present moment, even beyond the next few hours. We had survived this round, but the situation was still far from stable. I needed more than just a Plan A, B, or C. I needed an entire alphabet of contingency plans.

The rain had given us a reprieve, but I knew that leadership, especially in moments like these, was not about waiting for another lucky break. It was about staying three steps ahead, about anticipating the worst while hoping for the best. And with that thought, I quietly started mapping out the rest of the day in my mind, knowing full well that every drop of water, every grain of food, and every decision I made now could shape what tomorrow might bring.

Chapter - 30

Power in Crisis

By early noon, the UPS supporting our intercom system had given up. The once-reliable connection between us and the guests, as well as any outside communication through landlines, was severed. We were now effectively cut off, with no way to reach room guests, and more troublingly, no way for them to reach us. Our mobile phones, too, were on the brink of dying, drained from hours of use in an increasingly uncertain environment.

Questions started swirling in my mind like a storm: *What if there is an emergency? What if a guest needs urgent help and cannot make it all the way down? What about our elderly guests? How will we manage to attend to their needs if they can't reach us?*

The gravity of the situation was clear, but I had to find a solution. "*Put a help desk on each floor,*" I instructed the FOM.

He looked at me, puzzled, "*Sir, means?*"

"Internal communications are down, and the mobile numbers we've given the guests aren't much help either, since most of our phones, and theirs, are almost dead. We need a dedicated person on each floor to coordinate the needs of the guests directly." I was convinced this was the best way to maintain some semblance of contact.

But that still left us with another pressing issue, our dying mobile batteries.

With the weight of these thoughts pressing down on me, I walked out to the porch. The once-bustling city had come to a standstill, and the porch had become a gathering place for the guests, their makeshift refuge amid the chaos. The river water roared and swirled on the roads, transforming the landscape into what almost looked like the view from a riverside resort. I made a light-hearted remark to lift the mood, "*Shaher me resort ka maza,*" ("the ambience of a resort in a city hotel") and despite the situation, a few guests laughed. One even giggled, repeating, "*Resort ka maza, haan!*

But the stillness of the city was haunting. No sounds of traffic, no rescue boats from the authorities, just the steady droning of a car alarm from a vehicle submerged in water nearby. "*Kabse alarm baj raha hai, bahut tikau battery hai iski,*" ("the alarm has been buzzing for so long, seems it has a very durable battery") a guest murmured dryly.

And then it hit me, *battery!* That was the key. We had two hotel cars parked on the porch: their engines untouched by the rising floodwaters.

Without wasting a moment, I grabbed the keys and slid into the driver's seat of one of the cars. Plugging in my phone, I set it to charge and called for two more phones from my key team members. And I saw by now a few guests already started harboring in their own vehicles, for the same reason, to charge their phones and stay connected. I approached them and encouraged them to share their car chargers with other guests who did not have vehicles.

What followed was something remarkable. Crisis, I have often believed, has a way of teaching us discipline, and in this case, sense of community as well. Guests began forming an impromptu queue to charge their phones, no one pushing or shoving, each waiting: patiently for their turn. We opened our second hotel car for charging, allowing more people: to power up their phones, giving them the ability to inform worried family members of their safety. It was a small victory, but in such times, even the smallest of victories feel monumental.

As I was busy coordinating the charging stations, I noticed a jittery woman standing off to the side, clutching her phone in one hand and a small device, a power bank, in the other. She looked anxious, her eyes scanning the crowd as if searching for someone she could ask for help. But each time she opened her mouth, the words seemed to falter, retreating into her throat.

I walked over to her gently and asked, "*Can I assist you with anything?*" Before I could finish, she thrust her iPhone and power bank into my hands. "*M-my phhones battari is only 4%, ohhh, evvrryone att homee een my countari are soo soo worrid,*" she stammered in a thick accent, her voice trembling.

"*Don't worry,*" I reassured her. I pulled my phone, which had charged up to 70%, from the car and placed hers in its stead. Then, I asked a bell boy to keep an eye on the phones while they charged.

She introduced herself as Annie, a faculty of a medical college from Georgia (EU), here for an exchange program with one of Vadodara's universities. I happened to know Mr. Patel, the university's owner, and mentioning this seemed to bring her some comfort, a sense of security during this unfamiliar crisis. A few light-hearted dialogues, and she was soon smiling, forgetting about the floods, if only for a moment.

I assured her that my team and I would do everything in our power to keep everyone safe and minimize any inconveniences. She expressed her gratitude, not just for charging her phone, but for making her feel less alone in this ordeal. That is the thing about crises, they have a way of turning strangers into family, and a place that once felt unfamiliar into something resembling home.

As I watched guests quietly fall into the rhythm of sharing and supporting one another, I knew that this place had become more than just a hotel, it had become a household. And as the head of that household, I had many important tasks to oversee. Tasks that needed to be handled with care, with precision, and, most importantly, with heart.

With phones charging, and spirits lifted for now, I prepared myself for the next challenge. There would be many more to come, but with each one, I knew we were growing stronger, together.

Chapter – 31

A Boat, a Promise, and a War Cry

Although the phones were charging, it seemed the towers which were providing the network were mostly failing as it had been more than 24 hours, and there was no power in most of the city, so presumably the backup power of most of the IBS towers must have drained. But this was only the tip of the issue, the real problem was that most of the incoming or outgoing calls were dropping. Every time I would receive a call, it would be just enough of an intimation to know that someone was trying to reach me, but the connection would cut off before we could converse.

Somehow, when I was walking through the hotel, I realized that at a particular point between the 6th and 7th floors, I was able to talk and hear clearly without the calls dropping. Now, every time I had to make or receive a call, I had to climb up to that point, and without electricity and the elevator, it was becoming cumbersome. But I had to do what I had to do.

The water in the RO plant storage tank was only enough for a few more drinking water requests. But we needed water for so much more, for cooking dinner, providing for guests through the night and early morning, water for staff, and breakfast preparations. The need was endless, and the resources limited. My brain was working overtime, analyzing every possibility, every permutation of how we could arrange the water we needed.

A true leader helps others, yes, but what people forget is that a true leader also knows when to take help. I climbed the stairs to that sweet and strategic spot where the network worked and started dialing. One by one, I tried contacting anyone who could help, someone with better access, someone who could arrange water for us, or at least evacuate my guests and staff. But hope felt as slippery as water between my fingers. Some contacts managed to line up a truck of water, but it was stopped miles from the hotel by the police because of road closures and water levels.

I had assigned a few team members to dial 102, the emergency number, but every time they connected, the operators seemed too overwhelmed to help. Half-listened stories, tired and frustrated voices, and then, the line would go dead. The situation was spiraling downward, calls for help met with promises that never materialized, no boats, no rescue teams.

Our FOM, who had dealt with guest no-shows in daily operations, had never been so frustrated by the actual no-show of those who had promised rescue.

Finally, one call seemed to bear some fruit. A truck loaded with water bottles had made it within five kilometers of the hotel but was stopped at yet another blockade. I urged the truck driver to let me speak with the police officer in charge. In Gujarati, I pleaded with him: "*Sahib aawa deo eene, ayian ghana maanas fasayela che, beju badhu vastu ni vaat nathi, paani vagar keevi reete jeewshe?*" ("Sir, please let them come here, there are lot of people stuck here, other things could be left for, but how to survive without water"). My words poured out like a torrent of desperation, hoping my knowledge of the local language would break through.

But the officer, though calm, was firm. He explained that the water on the road was too deep, and no vehicle could cross it. "*Shaeb tarwi ne nai par tarni ne aawi shakay beejo rasto nathi,*"

("Sir it's not even possible to come by swimming, one can come by drowning only") he said and hung up.

"Swim." That was the word that lingered in my mind. Could I swim to the truck? Of course, I could as a swimmer, but what about bringing the water back to the hotel? I needed a plan.

And then, like a thunderbolt, it struck me. "*Boat!*" I shouted. Everyone around me looked bewildered. "*What?*" they echoed.

"*Boat!*" I repeated, more emphatically this time. "We'll build a boat. That is our Plan E, F, G, whatever, *but we must build a boat now!*"

Manu darted off to find the in-house carpenter and gather plywood floating around. We found some drums left from engine oil storage, and soon enough, the entire team, bellhop, housekeepers, engineers, and even some guests, gathered around to help. With ropes, tools, and a dose of ingenuity, we crafted a makeshift raft. The hotel's porch had turned into a scene from some guerrilla engineering show, with every hand working together to make our desperate plan a reality.

Building the boat was complete after an hour and a half of effort, a humble creation but solid enough to carry water. I felt like Archimedes, staring at a boat that could be our salvation. We started testing it on the water, it floated, but balance was an issue.

"*Sir, yeh humare baithne se disbalance ho rahi hai,*" ("Sir, it's getting off the balance as we are sitting on it") one of the plumbers remarked.

"*Yeh humare baithne ke liye nahi hai,*" ("This isn't meant for us to sit upon") I explained. "*This is for water bottles. We'll push it from behind like a handcart, with water bottles on top.*"

The boat was designed not for people but for cargo, our precious water bottles. We would drag it through the water to ferry supplies across the flooded streets.

Once the boat was ready, I made a few more calls, hoping to secure the water delivery again. But the truck had already left from the spot abandoning us in the realm of misery. The driver informed me that he was told not to enter the area and would not return until tomorrow morning, after 9 a.m. A heavy sigh rippled through the team. The delay felt like a blow to the gut. But I assured them that we now had a resource, a boat, ready for when the next opportunity presented itself.

Until then, we would wait. I instructed everyone to keep trying their contacts, to use every connection they had, and to keep the hope alive. Meanwhile, the guests, having finished their lunch, were oblivious to the struggle playing out behind the scenes. They relaxed, being assured, that everything was being taken care of.

I, however, felt the burden of the war of logistics weighing heavily on my shoulders. I pulled out a small, half-empty 200 ml water bottle from my thigh pocket. I realized that I had consumed barely 100 ml of water all day. Normally, I would drink five to six liters easily, but today, survival dictated a new rhythm. I stared at the remaining water, then gulped it down in one shot, crushing the bottle in my fist with a determined smile.

Turning to my team, I declared, "Today in the evening, I will drink a full Liter in one go. Until then, this was the last." It was not just a statement, it was a vow, a war cry, a promise to myself and everyone around me that I would not stop fighting. I would get us the water we needed. I would keep us all afloat.

Flooded Floors to Open Doors: A Sanctuary Reclaimed

Chapter - 32

The Weight of Trust

The air was thick with tension, and every drop of water we managed to secure was as precious as gold. FOM and FBM had been running around, contacting anyone they could to find water sources. FOM was tasked with arranging the logistics, while FBM searched for suppliers who still had a working establishment and could provide the copious quantities of water we needed. Every call felt like a step closer to survival, or a reminder of how close we were to failure.

But despite the continuous efforts, the responses were dispiritingly similar: "We have the water but getting it to you is impossible." The logistics issue was the devil, a shadowy force suffocating every glimmer of hope. I kept FOM & FBM on the job, urging them to keep trying. But deep down, I knew it was going to take more than persistence to break through.

Determined to stay ahead of the storm, I climbed once again to that elusive sweet spot between the sixth and seventh floors, where mobile signals seemed to dance on the edge of chaos, like a secret whisper in the wind. My phone buzzed just as I reached the top. It was FOM. For a brief, shining moment, I thought this might be the breakthrough for which I was waiting.

"Any success?" I asked, a flicker of hope lighting up my voice.

"Sir... there's a problem." His words smashed my castle of expectations into dust. The silence hung heavy between us, like the eye of the storm.

"Go on," I said, trying to keep my tone steady.

"Mr. Bhatia needs a doctor, he is consistently asking to arrange for a doctor," FOM explained. Mr. Bhatia was one of our long-staying guests, a kind but worried man who had been here with his wife. His wife, it turned out, was undergoing critical treatment, and she required time-bound injections, vital, lifesaving or life-changing injections. The clock was ticking, and there was no medical help in sight. FOM had tried to find a doctor, a nurse, anyone, but the roads were rivers, and the city had no lifeboats no rescue resources left.

The situation was a ticking time bomb. "Have you cross-checked the guest list for any medical professionals?" I asked. In moments like these, strength is not just about having resources; it is about knowing where to find them, sometimes within the very walls of your building. We had compiled a list of all guests earlier, noting their professions, any unique skills or potential vulnerabilities, medical conditions, comorbidities, physical limitations, anything that might help in times of crisis, or we had to proactively take care of. But despite combing through it again, no doctors or paramedics were among us.

I paused, weighing my options. Time was not our friend. The injections had to be administered by midnight, and two more were due the following morning. There was no room for failure.

"What will you do now?" I asked, my voice a mirror of the storm outside, restless, full of questions with no easy answers, *"that's why I called you sir, after I didn't get any success of getting doctor or nurse only thing that could strike in my mind was your name, I know you will beat this situation in a second"* FOM literally stocked boulder

of responsibility on my head. But it went on miraculously well, as someone reminds you of the power you have, and you suddenly become an alpha warrior.

My mind raced. The pressure was mounting like a tidal wave. FOM had exhausted all options. I was the last line of defense, and the weight of his expectation was heavy. But something inside me clicked, a warrior's instinct sharpened by years of crisis management. When a true leader faces impossible odds, they do not just give solutions, they become the solution.

"Sure, I'll handle this myself," I said, an iron resolve creeping into my voice. *"I am so sure, sir?"* he said, half in awe, half in utter belief.

"Tell Mr. Bhatia that the GM has taken over the matter. Now he's in safe hands."

I had to make sure everything was by the book. *"Do they have the prescription?"* I asked, knowing that every detail had to be in order.

"Yes, they do," FOM replied, sounding relieved. The message was conveyed to the Bhatias. *"Koi doctor nahi mil raha? Toh GM saab ko bol do, woh hi laga denge!"* ("If there is no doctor available, ask GM sir that he should administer the jab") Mr. Bhatia had joked to FOM, his voice filled with the kind of faith that comes from watching a leader in action. He had seen me battle one challenge after another, perhaps assuming if I could keep this fortress running amidst a flood, I could do anything.

What Mr. Bhatia did not know was that his comment was not extremely far from the truth. I had a secret weapon up my sleeve: I was a certified first-aider, trained in handling various medical emergencies, CPR, wound administration, anaphylaxis, including administering prescribed injections. In fact, I had experience doing so within my own family, having dealt with medical emergencies before. My training in survival techniques and crisis management made me the right person for the job, even though this situation was a different kind of battlefield.

"Let's hope GM sir hi lagaenge," ("Let's hope GM sir only will administer") FOM had said to Mr. Bhatia, half in jest, half in seriousness. But it was not a joke anymore. I was ready to step in but did keep FOM still at the task of finding the doctor or nurse.

As I prepared mentally for the task ahead, I could not help but reflect on the irony of it all. Amidst the chaos of floods, lack of resources, and an entire hotel full of people looking to me for leadership, I was about to do something incredibly personal. In a way, this was the simplest challenge I had faced in days, and yet, it was one of the most important.

A leader is not just someone who stands tall in the storm; they are the one who wades into the flood to pull you to safety, even if it means getting their hands dirty and feet murky.

——— --- ———

Flooded Floors to Open Doors: A Sanctuary Reclaimed

Chapter - 33

The Weight of Water

Time was slipping away, and there was still no respite in the efforts to secure water. Water for cooking dinner tonight, for breakfast tomorrow, and most crucially, water for all the guests and staff to drink, I again reminded myself. Late afternoon had come, yet there was not even a hint of hope. The FOM and FBM were relentless, their minds spinning through plans A, B, C, D, and on, but every plan seemed to slip like sultry silt through their hands, with time ticking away. Calculations, routes, pinpointing depots of water, none of it was yielding results.

Meanwhile, my own mind was a battlefield. The boat was ready, but it was not a solution until tomorrow morning. The water depots were too far off to reach tonight, and wading through floodwaters held not just the terror of potholes but also the unsettling risk of crocodiles swept in by the overflowing rivers. What else could I do? I murmured to myself, seeking answers from the depths of my mind. As the saying goes, survival is resourcefulness. A true leader, survivor, or savior must find solutions in every hidden crevice, and the weight on my shoulders was that I had to be all three.

I quietly rose from the parapet wall of the main porch and headed to the banquet's back area. I grabbed a bubble-top water dispenser and covered the tap's orifice with a clean muslin cloth. With sand buckets lying nearby for firefighting, I filled the dispenser with layers of sand, followed by charcoal from our coal storage, then more sand, then charcoal, and again sand, until the topmost layer was filled with gravel from a useless embankment nearby. **Voilà**—a makeshift sand-charcoal water filter was born. I quickly made another, intending to filter water through both.

Yet the challenge was not over. The water flowing around us was tainted with filth and pathogens; mere filtration would not suffice. It had to be disinfected. Luckily, our hotel, following HACCP (food safety) protocols, had chlorine dose tablets on hand for disinfecting vegetables, salads and other raw materials. I knew the exact dosage to turn untreated water into potable drinking water. This was **Plan H**.

It felt like a stroke of genius, but it was not enough. The treatment process would take too long to supply the volumes we needed for dinner or for guests to drink in the short term. This plan was now my last resort, a SOS solution for survival alone, not for the calm, composed environment I had worked so hard to maintain for the guests. I could not afford to induce panic.

I fielded more calls, yet none brought promising news. The options were there, but none brought assurance. With a heavy heart, I climbed to my room, hoping a moment of solitude might clear my mind. Should I pursue the sand-charcoal filter solution? Could I risk the taste of chlorine lingering in the guests' water? As these thoughts whirled in my mind, I opened the window of my room, lit a cigarette; though I wasn't a smoker, but for these days I was using it just as a placebo for resting or a short break, and stared down at the raging river Viswamitri like a war commander locking eyes with his rival.

As I scanned the chaos, my gaze landed on the roof of a bungalow in the nearby Samrajya society. There was a large plastic water tank, tilted and fallen. "What a waste," I murmured, feeling the weight of missed opportunities. If I had a spare tank like that, I would have been in a vastly different situation.

And then, suddenly the realization came. **Water tank!** One minute! I leaned out of the window, glancing right. There was a building next door, rented by the hotel to house our finance office and records. A white pipe was connected from our hotel's treated water storage tank to the overhead tank (OHT) of that building.

Without wasting a second, I grabbed my phone and called the FBM. He answered with cautious hope. "Sir, water may be arranged, chances are 50-50. But the confirmation will come after two hours," he said. **Two hours**? In this crisis, two hours was an eternity. We needed water now to cook before darkness fell, with no electricity to light our way.

I said, *"Keep trying, but I've got a **Plan J**. We will have enough water to cook dinner and provide drinking water for some guests with minimal processing."*

"Sir!! How? Are authorities finally coming to help?" FBM asked, his voice amazed.

"No, the highest authority has provided," I said, pointing to the sky as if to suggest divine intervention. "But the answer was right next door."

"Salute to you, sir," he responded, breathless with disbelief.

I rushed downstairs, my heart pounding with urgency. "Chef, we have secured water. Get the entire kitchen and service staff here, now!" Within minutes, the team had assembled. I explained the plan. "We will form a human chain, taking utensils into Samrajya society. We will enter through the front door of our accounts building and fill the containers from the water in the OHT."

The realization hit everyone like a revelation, they could not believe that such an obvious solution had eluded them, and even I was amused by my heedlessness. There were gasps of amazement and looks of relief, but there was no time for awe. "Move now!" I yelled, and the team was off, a well-oiled machine in motion.

I instructed the chef to boil at least 50 liters of water. While the water from our WTP was fit to drink, I wanted no risks. Medical help was too far, and I was not about to gamble on anyone's health, especially the elderly and children among us.

The brigade of boys was triumphant, carrying water as if they had seized a treasure from the enemy lines. Every single one of them proudly flaunted their possession of water, their morale restored.

The situation, for now, was under control. We had conquered yet another challenge, this one through sheer ingenuity and teamwork. It was a **cumulative victory**, and most importantly, it was my team's.

Chapter - 34

The Siege of Survival

It was almost dusk, and though the discovery of water in our office building had eased the pressure significantly, the battle was far from over. I did not want to cease the pursuit of securing enough water, knowing the situation could easily escalate again. The FOM had finally managed to contact a tractor vendor, experienced in wading through the floodwaters. He knew a way to reach a place where we could access a water depot. It was a breakthrough.

The person at the depot had begun filling water jugs, 20 liters each, but it would take at least two hours for him to fill enough for us. The FBM, who had taken on the task of fetching the water, was on his way, ensuring that the precious consignment would arrive safely. However, there was one challenge: we had to return all the empty jugs by morning. How could we possibly consume all that water overnight? I thought about it briefly and pushed the concern aside, **let's get the water here first**, I told myself.

On the porch, guests had gathered, gazing at the water, which was lapping back and forth like a restless sea. They were deep in discussion, trying to make sense of what fate had in store for them. As I approached, they respectfully parted, making way for me. I made my way to the end of the ramp, where the water threatened us like an encroaching tide.

*"**GM saab, kya lagta hai, paani kam hua ya badha hai?**"* ("GM sir, what do you think, the water level has increased or receded") a couple of guests asked, hopeful but anxious. I squatted down, switched on my high-beam torch, and pointed to a spot in the distance.

"Woh jo light dikh rahi hai, pehle paani usko touch kar raha tha, ab dekho; aadha inch neeche hai," ("Do you see that light fitting, previously the water was touching it, and now look it's half an inch below") I said.

Their relief was palpable. There were murmurs of joy as they absorbed this simple but powerful fact. *"Don't worry, tomorrow morning will be a **Good Morning**,"* I said, my tone firm and assuring.

For the next hour, I became a sort of living record, repeating the same scenario over and over. Each time a guest came to me with the same question, I would point to the light and explain the half inch of receding water, always ending with the same hopeful phrase. The repetition did not bother me; it was what they needed. Calm spreads like fire, and I was happy to fan the flames of confidence.

After ensuring my core team members were relieved for dinner, I checked on the dinner layout for the staff and then made my way to the restaurant. The scene inside was like something out of a peaceful hamlet, **another candlelight dinner** with a humble buffet. Guests chatted and assured each other, their morale soaring. As I walked by, I overheard a lady speaking to Annie, boosting her spirits. *"I understand your situation, dear. I can imagine what you are going through..."* said the lady to her.

It warmed my heart to witness the hope spreading. **High morale is contagious**, I thought. As a leader, if you can inspire a few minds, they will pass that energy on many others.

"GM saab, aap bhi dinner kar lo, 9 baj gaye hain," ("GM sir, you also have dinner please, its already past nine") came a voice from behind. Startled, I turned to see Mr. and Mrs. Bhatia, smiling as they finished their meal.

I smiled back. *"I have a specific ritual to follow before dinner. After a long day like this, I need to relax a bit, but I cannot afford to do so tonight. I have an important task at midnight, and I cannot risk falling into a deep sleep."*

Mr. Bhatia nodded, understanding the situation, and taking cognizance that I had to either arrange for a doctor or must act like one for vital injection dose to be given to Mrs Bhatia. He shook my hand, offering his gratitude before he and his wife headed to their room.

After handling a few more briefings here and there, I stepped out onto the porch and got a call from FBM. The connection was poor, but I managed to make out fragments: *"Water... jugs... reaching... hotel..."*

I immediately called the chef and rallied the team for one more battle. The tractor arrived; its front tires lifted in the air as the rear tires struggled through the floodwaters. The team sprang into action, forming a human chain. The first group passed the jugs from the trolley to the porch, the second group moved them from the porch to the lobby, and a final team hauled them up the stairs, handing off the jugs at each turn. Within minutes, all 40 jugs were safely on the terrace.

I instructed the team to pour the water into the RO water tank, ensuring it would be distributed evenly throughout the hotel. This also allowed us to control the storage better. I did not want any jugs lying around by morning, everything had to be organized to avoid another hustle at dawn.

We kept 10 jugs in the restaurant, and the team collected empty bottles from guests, refilling them with fresh water. For now, the **water problem has been solved**, at least by tomorrow evening. I glanced at the clock, it was already 11 p.m. I grabbed a bottle of water, finished it in one swift gulp, and crushed it in my hand like a marine commando neutralizing a threat.

It was not over yet. I called Manu for debrief and assigned tasks for the morning to my lead team members, and then picked up my box of **khichdi** and pickle. But I had one more task: a visit to Mr. Bhatia's room at midnight.

By now, Mr. Bhatia had left 2-3 reminders at the front desk to make sure we would not forget about the task of injection. My body had become a walking alarm clock, and right at 11:55 p.m., I was at Mr. Bhatia's door, a bottle of sanitizer in one hand and a mask on my face. I knocked, and he welcomed me in.

With the emergency torch I had brought, I checked the prescription, prepared the vial, and chatted with Mrs. Bhatia as I disinfected the surface skin. **Prick!** The needle went in, and I gently administered the medication. As I pulled out the needle and disinfected her skin again, I joked, *"That must have been the worst jab ever?"*

"Nooo! Do not tell me you were not a doctor before becoming a GM!" Mrs. Bhatia exclaimed, impressed by my steady hand and dexterity of the administration of injection. I laughed, sharing a few stories from my schooling and the training I had received over the years. Mr. Bhatia, a hotelier himself, said, *"I knew there was something different about you. I own many hotels, and I've dealt with plenty of GMs, but you're different."*

"Maybe it's the crisis, that I am acting differently, or your point of view has become different" I replied with a chuckle, adding a humorous satire to lighten the mood. After bidding them goodnight, I finally retired for the day.

Exhausted, I freshened up with half a liter of water. My feet ached from hours of running up and down in heavy gumboots. I pulled the curtains back and stood by the window with my **khichdi**, gazing at the river's waters under the bright twilight. As I savored each bite, I felt a sense of victory rising within me, as if mocking the river: **You may have taken two days. and nights from us, but tomorrow, the day will be ours. We will rise and rise, and we will not bow to your rise.**

Flooded Floors to Open Doors: A Sanctuary Reclaimed

Chapter - 35

Dawn of Relief

It was late in the night when I finally sank into bed, bracing myself for another brief rest yet alert. I placed a pillow under my back, a subtle reminder to stay vigilant and ready, even in sleep. Moments later, exhaustion claimed me; the mental and physical toll of the day blurred my thoughts, and I drifted off. The steady thump of my own heartbeat became a comforting rhythm as I let go of the day's burdens.

An hour or so passed just before I stirred awoke, and muscles taut with a residual readiness. Tired body was having reflexes as if every part were trying to involuntarily jump into the mission, and heart was pulsating heavily like a racing car revving in rage. I knew what was happening, I needed to calm myself down, so started murmuring a few mantras softly, chanting "Jai Shree Ram" and "Om Namah Shivaya" in reverence and rhythm, feeling them wrap around me like a protective shroud. The power of those words; it is unique about them, they are amazingly adaptive as per the emotional status or rather need of a person, it is like equal parts as war cry and equally a lullaby too, it began to soothe my nerves. My heartbeat softened, the air around me grew still, and I slipped back into a peaceful slumber, sheltered by the ancient weight of faith.

When morning's light finally broke through the window, I felt its tentative warmth against my eyelids. My body protested as I pulled myself up, my eyes heavy as if weighed by sandbags. I staggered toward the window with a vision still blurred from sleep, rubbing my eyelashes to clear the haze. There it was, the river, swollen and relentless as ever. My heart shattered at the sight. I had been so sure that today would bring relief, a lowering of water levels.

But then, just as disappointment began to settle and so did the haze from my analytical vision, I noticed something, the river's ferocity had diminished. The expanse of water stretching toward Akota seemed narrower than before, and though its level remained high, the current was visibly weaker. Relief washed over me like a balm, warming my spirit. This was heartening news, something to hold onto. I dressed quickly, slipping into a fresh pair of camo battle gear, and made my way downstairs with purpose.

The hotel's porch bore the first signs of emerging from its watery siege; the water had receded significantly, leaving dirt and debris scattered everywhere. The road was partially visible again, strewn with remnants of the flood, a chilling reminder of nature's might.

Among the detritus was the carcass of a cow, lodged against the rear tire of a car. A somber sight, a stark reminder of what the river had taken and displaced.

Inside, the guests who had been stranded with us were stirring, eager to resume their interrupted journeys. A few early birds were already seated in the restaurant, savoring *the breakfast* that tasted like hope. People began checking out, paying in cash or via UPI, our choice to conserve battery-operated payment systems was proving invaluable now. Smiling faces, clasped hands, and murmurs of gratitude filled the lobby, each goodbye a small victory, a farewell laden with recognition of our efforts to keep them safe and steady.

Amid the farewells, Annie's transport arrived. Her hosts from university were here, ready to take her to safer ground. She folded her hands in a tearful but joyful *namaste*, then hugged me with a brief, silent gratitude that said everything. Sometimes, crisis weave a web of connections you would never expect; bonds forged in the fires of survival do not fade quickly. Her parting gesture was not just a farewell; it was a silent nod to the entire team, a gesture, that spoke of shared strength and resilience.

The dawn of relief had come, not just for the guests, but for all of us, especially the ones who had weathered the storm from within.

Chapter - 36

The Aftermath of the Deluge

The floodwaters had receded, leaving behind not just a waterlogged city but a hotel in dire need of recovery. While the raging Viswamitri River had retreated, its remnants: sludge, debris, and silence cumulatively lingered like the aftermath of a storm. The new struggle was abreast and far from over.

I began my rounds, inspecting areas that had been submerged and inaccessible until now. The damage assessment was crucial for restarting the operations. My first stop was the raw power supply. As expected, the city was still reeling, with no electricity restored. Yet, amidst this, one thing stood as a testament to resilience: the uninterrupted gas line supply. While I had ensured we had enough LPG cylinders for at least a week, the steady PNG supply was a blessing, sparing us one less worry.

Next, I inspected the diesel generator (DG) set. Opening its service door, my fears were confirmed, the tainted watermarks showed the floodwaters had reached the alternator. The batteries were drenched, rendering the DG inoperative. It would take more than quick fixes to revive it. Without hesitation, I called Mr. Agarwal, one of the directors, whose experience with a flood-prone hotel had made him an expert in such crises. I requested a pump and a small portable DG set to jumpstart our basic operations. His understanding and swift response were reassuring.

The basement was another matter. Sludgy water filled every corner, creating a daunting scene of muck and murk. My team started working tirelessly to clean and clear submerged areas. In the meantime, I arranged for a fresh supply of bottled water and a water tanker since the Water Treatment Plant (WTP) remained compromised.

As I stood on the porch, directing operations, I saw the HR Manager arriving. Handing him the responsibility of staff welfare and logistics, I allowed myself a moment of relief, knowing I could focus on the larger challenges at hand.

Moments later, my eyes fell on a familiar figure entering the lobby: Mr. Amit Momaya, our Regional Finance Controller. His presence was a godsend. Our connection had been severed during the flood due to network failures, and now, with his arrival, I felt a wave of reassurance. Mr. Amit's diligence and ability to tackle intricate tasks freed me to concentrate on immediate priorities. With just a handshake, we communicated everything, our shared resolve to conquer the chaos and rebuild order from this watery devastation.

As we strategized, I received a call from Mr. KP, the General Manager of another hotel in our group that had been untouched by the flood. His words were firm, his intent unwavering:

"I'll be there shortly. I know you don't have a Chief Engineer. I'm bringing mine, along with a three-phase submersible pump for you."

This was not the end of the outpouring of support. Mr. Shah, another director, called to inform me that his son, Mr. Karan, was already combing the market for portable diesel pumps and other essential equipment. The chain of assistance and camaraderie from all quarters; colleagues, directors, and friends, it felt like the universe's way of rewarding our unyielding efforts.

Standing there, I realized this was not just about managing resources; it was about rallying every ounce of determination, teamwork, and goodwill we could muster. This was not merely a recovery, it was a resurgence, a testament to the resilience of the human spirit and the strength of collective resolve.

Flooded Floors to Open Doors: A Sanctuary Reclaimed

Chapter - 37

The Race to Recovery

The day had dawned with streaks of hope scattered across the landscape. Everywhere, signs of life were returning, people hauling their belongings back to homes that had withdrawn from the clutches of the flood, shopkeepers inspecting the damage, families scrubbing floors and basements to reclaim their spaces. The streets, a picture of chaos, were alive with the energy of rescue vehicles and laborers. Beneath the surface of the bustle, there was a shared sentiment: hope, yet faint but resolute.

Inside the hotel, I stood amidst the activity, my mind racing like a high-powered processor. I listed out the essentials to bring the hotel back to life for our guests:

1. Seamless Power
2. Clean Water
3. Functional Elevators

Without these, the idea of reopening the hotel was a distant dream. Prioritizing clarity over burdening tasks and looking for most urgent jobs, I analyzed each task for its challenges and devised a plan.

The Power Plan

The existing DG set, submerged and incapacitated, was no longer dependable. I needed a standby generator to manage operations and prepare for the inevitable fluctuations once the raw power was restored. A call was placed, and arrangements began for a suitable-sized DG. At the same time the service center was informed about the damage and repair call was locked.

Water Woes

The WTP was still down, as it was in the basement which also housed motors vital for pumping water to the overhead tanks. But both were buried under few lakh liters of water mixed with thick sludge. Dewatering the basement was an immediate priority.

Elevators in Limbo

The elevator pits, obviously, were flooded and needed dewatering and cleaning before any repairs could begin. This task was critical to restoring guest comfort and operational efficiency.

Reinforcements Arrive

Just as I was formulating strategies, Mr. KP arrived with his engineering team and a powerful 7 HP, three-phase motor. Their presence was a morale booster. We deliberated on the best way to begin dewatering, finally deciding to use the lift shaft to access the water. The setup was quick, and the pump roared to life. But as the water flowed, it became evident that the motor's capacity was not enough for the vast volume of water.

The City Recce

Determined to expedite the process, KP and I ventured into the city to locate a higher- capacity pump. The streets resembled a dewatering festival, everywhere, pumps were working tirelessly, draining out flooded basements. After multiple stops and negotiations, we finally found a pump operator willing to help. He promised to arrive after 9 PM and we quickly agreed on rates as well as the time.

Night Operations

True to his word, the operator arrived late at night with the much needed 'dunki' pump. Assembling and setting up the equipment took nearly an hour, but once it started, the powerful gush of water gave us hope. The pump's efficiency was remarkable, and we estimated considerable progress by morning.

After ensuring everything was in place, I checked on the operator, arranging tea and snacks to keep him energized. I took a bucket of water from the water tanker and retreated to my room with a modest food packet for dinner.

A Quiet Feast

Freshened up and offering prayers, I sat quietly in the corner of my room to savor the simple meal. Exhaustion was clinging to my every muscle, but there was an underlying satisfaction, a sense of small victories and a remarkable breakthrough in a battle which was over, but the rehabilitation was pending. Battles do not just end on the day of truce or permanent ceasefire, they are lit like a burning piece of charcoal under the heap of ashes, and they remain like that until all the damage and destruction is not recovered. Which ideally never does, but at least for the face value of it. Although my body was weary, my mind was still galloping, leaping ahead to tomorrow's goals.

Sliding into the duvet, I closed my eyes and whispered, "Tomorrow will be a day of achievement. We'll tackle each task, one by one, and reclaim what's ours."

With that thought, I allowed myself to drift into the solace of much-needed sleep, ready to face the dawn of a new chapter in recovery.

Flooded Floors to Open Doors: A Sanctuary Reclaimed

Chapter - 38

The Price of Progress

The morning greeted me with aching limbs and a body weighed down by the consequences of relentless toil. Both ankles felt twisted, toes and fingers had developed a hematoma-like pigmentation, a silent testament to the toll of heavy gumboots and countless steps over the past days. Yet, there was no time to dwell on the pain. Limping but determined, I readied myself for another day of tackling the hotel's recovery.

Descending the stairs with a measured but steady gait, I paused to exchange quick words of motivation and gratitude with every team member I encountered. Their weary faces lit up with renewed energy. At the main porch, Mohsin, one of our valets, noticed my limp.

"Sir, chot lag gayi kya?" ("Sir! are you hurt") he asked, concern etched on his face.

I chuckled, replying with a metaphorical jest, *"Nai re! Engine garam ho raha hai, thodi der mein dekhna superspeed se chalega."* ("No! the engine is getting warmed; you will see in no time it will be at its top speed"). He laughed, and that light moment set a positive tone for the day.

Shifting Priorities

The basement was now accessible, though still ankle-deep in water. Progress had been made, but the enormity of the task ahead loomed large. Small pumps were now needed to drain the remaining water, a time-consuming process. However, my focus shifted to the hotel's water tanks. These were at ground level and untouched by the floodwaters, but I could not risk contamination.

Halting the basement dewatering efforts temporarily, I directed the team to focus on the tanks. Chlorinating the water heavily, I ensured it was safe for cleaning purposes. The process was swift, using the chlorinated water to scrub the tank interiors and surrounding areas. As I stood by watching the team at work, it felt like a moment of satisfaction, two problems addressed in one go.

The Big Leap

Next, I coordinated with Mr. Momaya to procure two 7 HP submersible pumps. When I announced this plan to the team, a surprise was evident.

"Such huge capacity pumps, and submersible!! sir?" someone asked, curious.

I explained, "These pumps will not only refill our overhead tanks swiftly but also act as a safeguard in future floods, ensuring we have a robust water supply system in place."

With Mr. Momaya's efficiency in procurement and the diligent work of Manu and Rakesh, our plumber, the pumps were quickly installed. By evening, the tanks were replenished with water supplied by municipal corporation, treated with chlorine, tested for the needed PPM as well as TDS, and ready to supply the overhead tanks. Soon enough, the water supply resumed, followed by clean water for the kitchen, thanks to our RO water plant which was situated on the top floor.

Building Momentum

With one major task checked off the list, I left the arrangements for the backup DG set in Mr. Momaya's capable hands and turned my attention to sanitation efforts and the further dewatering of the basement and lift pits.

The day felt like a whirlwind of activity, calculated actions, precise decisions, and unwavering coordination. Every step required meticulous planning, as one misstep could derail the delicate balance I had been striving to achieve.

As the day wore on, fatigue began to creep in. But the sight of progress, my team moving like clockwork, tanks refilled, and systems coming back online: kept my resolve intact. The road to full recovery was still long, but for the first time in days, I felt like the hotel was inching closer to reclaiming its former glory.

Complacency was not an option; and vigilance had always been my mantra. With every completed task, the horizon of possibilities grew brighter. Tomorrow would be another day of challenges, but I knew we were getting closer to achieving a sense of normalcy, with one deliberate step at a time.

Flooded Floors to Open Doors: A Sanctuary Reclaimed

Chapter - 39

Restoring Heights

The day began with my body reminding me of every mile walked, every weight lifted, and every task endured over the past week. My ankles protested with sharp stabs of pain, and my toes bore the pigmentation and sores of fatigue, a testament to the gumboots' unyielding yet crucial grip during long hours of labour. Despite the soreness, I dragged myself ahead to complete my morning routines; determined to push forward.

The warm cascade of water from the shower felt like a reunion with an old friend, washing away not just grime but a fraction of the fatigue that had seeped into my bones. After days of makeshift hygiene routines, this shower felt almost ceremonial, a moment of solace amid the chaos. Though my body still bore the strain, my resolve grew firmer with each passing moment.

Dressed and ready, I descended to the basement to assess the progress. With most of the water now removed, the space was exposed for what it had become, a pit of sludge, rotting debris, and remnants of the flood's havoc. The air was heavy with the stench of decay, and highly humid palpation, a constant reminder of nature's fury.

Yadav, our former stores in-charge, stood at the forefront, rallying laborers, and coordinating logistics to clear the basement. His decision to step in, despite having left the organization, spoke volumes about his respect and commitment to the institution. Watching him work alongside the team with such unwavering dedication was both humbling and inspiring.

Several buckets of sludge were removed, and the foul remnants of rotting food were carefully segregated for disposal. The combined effort of the team began to transform the basement.

Manu and I turned our attention to the lift pits, where water stubbornly lingered. Equipped with a wet vacuum cleaner and halogen lights, we tackled the pits floor by floor, meticulously drying each component.

Hours passed, each one blending into the next, until the pits were finally cleared. The elevator technician arrived, and the wait began as he conducted a series of rigorous checks. Every sensor, fail-safe mechanism, and control system were inspected with surgical precision.

Finally, the elevators hummed back to life. The sound was music to my ears, an achievement born from persistence and teamwork.

With the elevators operational in the late evening, I gave the go-ahead to the Front Office Manager to announce that we were ready for business. It was a declaration of victory, a sign that the worst was behind us.

Then something happened, as if the universe wanted to mark the moment, I received a message from Mr. Dhawan, a long-time guest. *"Total chaos… My Mumbai to Vadodara flight cancelled. Managed to get on a Mumbai-Ahmedabad flight at 8 PM. Then three hours in a cab from Ahmedabad to Vadodara,"* he wrote.

Knowing he would arrive late, I called the FOM. *"Let Mr. Dhawan know we have a room ready, although breakfast might be limited."* Mr. Dhawan's gratitude was immediate, his faith in us a quiet reminder of why we had pushed so hard to reopen. His loyalty felt like an endorsement of all our efforts, a silent pat on the back from a familiar face.

As the night deepened, I conducted one final inspection. The HSD supply was sufficient, every area was checked and rechecked, and the premises had started to resemble the hotel we once knew. Satisfied, I picked up my small parcel of food again and returned to my room.

Sitting at the edge of the bed, I ate in silence, savoring not just the meal but the quiet pride of having rebuilt what the flood had tried to break. My body still ached, but my spirit was lighter, elated and relaxed at the same time. The road ahead was long, but tonight, there was peace.

Sliding under the duvet, I allowed myself to relish the moment. This was a victory, not just for me, but for the team, the guests, and the institution. With a peaceful mind, a smile on my face, and gratitude in my heart, I drifted into a deep, well-deserved sleep.

Chapter - 40

The Symphony of Revival

The morning sun poured through the grand glass doors of the lobby, casting golden streaks over the marble flooring, now polished clean and gleaming out of its flood-induced recklessness. The air inside was different today, not just because it was free of the damp, musty smell of days past, but because it was buzzing with life, hope, and celebration. For the first time in week, the hotel's heart, the lobby, was alive with the gentle buzz of patrons.

Where once the lobby had been sadly prosaic, a mere space of function amidst the crisis, it was now transformed into a scene of warmth and conviviality. Soft instrumental music floated through the air, blending harmoniously with the chatter of guests enjoying their coffee and the rhythmic clinking of cutlery from the breakfast area.

I stood quietly at one corner, observing. The front office desk had returned to its usual busy self, with guests checking in and out, their conversations peppered with expressions of gratitude and relief. The staff, though visibly tired, wore their brightest smiles, exuding the professionalism that had carried them through this challenging week.

"Sir, the insurance company's assessor is here," came a gentle reminder from our FOM, interrupting my moment of quiet observation. I nodded and made my way towards the guest elevator, which was now fully functional, a testament to the days of toil spent dewatering the pits, drying components, and ensuring every safety measure was in place.

The insurance walkthrough was an elaborate affair I was joined by Mr. Momaya, as he will later be the total in-charge of the process. We led the assessor to all the affected areas, pointing out the basement where sludge still lingered in stubborn corners, the kitchens that bore scars of water damage, and the utility spaces where equipment had suffered. Every photo taken, every note scribbled, felt like a step towards long-term recovery.

But the day was not just about inspections and claims.

Back-End Rebirth

The back-of-the-house was abuzz with activity. Teams worked tirelessly to clean and rehabilitate storage areas, cold rooms, and utility spaces. Yadav, our former store in charge, who had volunteered to manage the coordination of laborers and logistics. His calm yet commanding presence was a boon, and his loyalty leaving me humbled.

"Sir, this debris will take at least twenty trips to get cleared entirely," Yadav informed me as we assessed the mess. Piles of rotting food materials, broken crates, and water-damaged inventory cluttered the spaces. The stench was overwhelming, but the team's focus never wavered.

"We'll get it done," I assured him, appreciating his unwavering commitment.

Moments of Hope

By late afternoon, I found myself back in the lobby. A couple of regular guests, clearly pleased with the revived ambiance, approached me.

"You've done a phenomenal job, sir," said Mr. Mathur, one of our longtime patrons. *"This hotel is not just a place; it's an experience, and you've preserved that even in the face of calamity."*

His words filled me with quiet pride. Every drop of sweat, every sleepless night felt validated in that moment.

Documenting the Journey

Later, with a mobile camera in hand, I began documenting the state of the hotel. From the pristine lobby to the still-recovering back areas, every frame told a story of resilience and revival. These images were not just for insurance purposes, they were for us, a reminder of what we had overcome together.

As the day turned to evening, the lobby remained a hub of soft commotion. The staff, though exhausted, kept the rhythm alive. The sound of laughter, the tapping of keyboards at the reception, and the clink of glasses at the café filled the air.

Standing at the entrance, I looked out at the city beyond. Streets were bustling again, vendors called out their wares, and the horizon held a promise of recovery. Inside the hotel, the orchestra of revival played on.

As night fell, I took a final round of the premises, inspecting every corner with habitual precision. The day had been long, but it ended with a profound sense of achievement. Back in my room, yet again with my same little, humble food parcel, I reflected on the transformation of the day, the lobby that had gone from muted to musical, the team that had risen above fatigue, and the guests whose smiles reminded me of the spirit we had upheld.

Sleep came easily that night, a peaceful surrender to a job well done. Tomorrow, I knew, would bring more challenges, but tonight was a celebration, a moment to bask in the triumph of today. *The triumph was ours and was reclaimed and robust.*

To establish a connection of hope and assurance I sent a message to our communication group in which all the promotors and stake holders were present.

"1st guest checked in at 1230 Midnight. Congratulations to all of us. Thank you all for the support, Prayers and the immense trust and faith in me.

I know it's an early celebration and there is too much to be taken care of and so many tasks in hand. But after a week-long turmoil

*It's a **good chant** of harbinger to say.*

WE ARE OPEN FOR BUSINESS!!!

Chapter - 41

Faith, Family, and Farewell *(The Missing Chapter)*

After days of relentless dedication, I realized there was one thing I had not fully attended to: *my family*. The reason wasn't that I was nonchalant about it, I had left home with proper pre-emptive measures and was constantly aware of the well-being of everyone at home. This only gives us a gaze at how our brave soldiers are committed on far away perilous and inhospitable borders, all focus on the mission, with keeping a solace of mere cognizance, a hope and prayer for the family. I had also, throughout the ordeal, carefully managed to shield them from the true gravity of the situation, painting a picture of manageable challenges while keeping them reassured.

My wife had been my silent support, her worry often masked with cheerful concern. *"Wahan toh sab theek hai na? Tumhare aas-paas toh paani nahi, hai na?"* ("I hope everything is alright there. Hope there is no inundation around your area") she would ask repeatedly, her voice slightly betraying the calm she tried to exude. Luckily or unfortunately all the news feeds including social media had seemingly disowned Vadodara floods and there was no news whatsoever anywhere, maybe because of power failures or network disruptions but there was total social media or news blackout. I had been careful never to let on just how precarious things had been, knowing her anxiety would double if she knew the truth.

"Photos bhejna," ("Do share photographs") she would insist every now and then, demanding to know the situation of water inundation around the area, not aware of the fact that the small waterlogging is a flood laden city now. *"We shouldn't take fun element in this, many people must be suffering,"* I eventually said firmly. It was

important for her to understand that this was not a situation for amusement but one requiring patience and resolve.

My 10-year-old daughter, Suvira, was no less worried, though she expressed her concern in her own unique way. She would call daily and often remind me, *"Papa, daredevil mat bano! Pani me jaane ki zarurat nahi hai, aur crocodiles ko pakadne ki koshish mat karna!"* ("Papa, don't be a daredevil, and no need to scout in deep waters, and ensure you don't try to catch or crocodiles")

Her admonitions were fuelled by her recent observations. Just a few weeks ago, she had seen a picture of me carefully lifting and rescuing a snake near the hotel's periphery. The area was teeming with staff, and the panic was palpable, but I had calmly maneuvered the snake into a drain where it could find safety. This was not an isolated incident; she had often seen me rescuing creatures like lizards, chameleons, bats stuck in households, without hesitation.

These episodes had left an impression on her, and now she was worried for my well-being.

I avoided video calls with her under the pretext of saving battery, which was although true, but it also shielded her from seeing the toll that every day would take on me. My tiredness, my sunken eyes, and my bruised hands were not what a father should show to his child who looks up to him as a pillar of strength. Although I would flaunt my every injury with pride jokingly saying *"assi ghav lage tan pe, fir bhi vyatha nahin man me"* ("Body got 80 wounds on, still the mind has pleasant tone"), but being still into the affair of chaos and away from her would make her terribly worried.

Despite the challenges, the days passed swiftly as the hotel began to chirp with cautious life again. On the twelfth day, it was Ganesh Chaturthi, day of renewal and reverence. For the occasion, we planned for Lord Ganesh's idol to be installed in the hotel. The hall at top, which had borne the air of despair not long ago and was confidante of all the staff who were taking their temporary refuge there, was now alive with the sound of prayers and the fragrance of flowers.

As I led the main prayer, a sense of calm washed over me. This was no ordinary celebration; it was a collective offering of gratitude, a testimony to the resilience of everyone who had endured this journey together. After the rituals, I distributed prasad to all, my heart full of both relief and reverence.

"Sir, do hafton se ghar nahi gaye ho. Sir, ghar kab jaoge?" ("Sir, it has been two weeks since you had gone home, when will you visit your home") one of the staff members asked with genuine concern.

I looked at him with a smile, my faith stronger than ever. *"Ab Ganpati Maharaj aa gaye hain, sabka aur hotel ka dhyan rakhne ke liye. Ab main aaram se ja sakta hoon ghar,"* ("Now Lord Ganpati has arrived, He will take care of the hotel, I can leave for home peacefully") I said with deep conviction and utter reverence.

With Lord Ganesh presiding over the hotel and its journey forward, I knew it was time to return to where I belonged from a long time: *home.*

That evening, I packed my belongings, walked through the lobby for one last inspection, and bid the team farewell. As I stepped out, I glanced at the building I had fiercely protected and nurtured. The road to full recovery would be long, but for now, stability had been achieved, and I could finally rest knowing the hotel was in safe hands.

Driving back, the city felt both familiar and changed, streets that were once underwater now carried the marks of resilience. When I reached home, my family welcomed me with open arms. Suvira ran to hug me tightly, and my wife's eyes spoke a thousand unspoken words of relief and peace, everyone was in literal tears as if a soldier had been retrieved from a deadly mission.

That night, for the first time in weeks, I slept in my own bed, at peace, surrounded by those who mattered most, with gratitude in my heart for the journey we had all endured.

Flooded Floors to Open Doors: A Sanctuary Reclaimed

Chapter - 0

Lessons from the Storm
A Guide to Resilience

In the aftermath of a crisis as monumental as the flood, the lessons we learned can became tools for survival and a testament to human ingenuity and perseverance. This chapter serves not only as a recounting of those days but as a practical guide for anyone facing similar challenges. From innovative solutions to emotional resilience, here are the key takeaways that helped us navigate the flood and emerge stronger.

1) Emotional Resilience: Finding Strength Amid Chaos

Crisis reveals the spectrum of human emotions. From fear and frustration to hope and determination, emotions can either paralyze or propel us forward.

- **Staying Positive:** Humor lightens the heaviest burdens. Whether joking with team members about a limp or exchanging light-hearted banter, laughter became a balm.

- **Managing Family Dynamics:** Shielding loved ones from the brunt of the crisis helped preserve their peace. I avoided video calls with my daughter Suvira to prevent her from seeing my exhaustion, instead choosing to convey calm through texts, audio calls and reassurances. This not only ensures the emotional well-being of family but also helps in minimizing the distraction from perpetual out of concern panic calls.

- **Empathy as Leadership:** Recognizing the struggles of the team and offering gratitude, encouragement, or a kind gesture kept morale high.

2) Practical Solutions: Survival Through Innovation

Necessity is the mother of invention, and in a crisis, quick thinking often becomes the difference between chaos and control.

- **Cooling Without Power:** With power supply intermittent, cooling rooms for guests and staff was a challenge. Drawing curtains apart to allow outside cooling to regulate temperature inside. Modulation in food also became a supplementary factor.

- **Charging Essentials:** Dead phones can mean dead communication. We charged phones devices using car batteries, ensuring that critical communication devices remained functional.

- **Water Filtration:** With water supplies compromised, we improvised a basic filtration system by layering sand, charcoal, and cloth in large vessels to remove impurities. Chlorination ensured it was safe to use.

- **Light in Darkness:** Using halogen lights to dry flooded elevator components showcased how even simple tools can have crucial roles when deployed strategically.

3) Safety Measures: Navigating Hazards

Safety took precedence in every decision. Floodwater brings a host of risks, from contamination to predating wildlife.

- **Avoiding Direct Contact with Water:** Using heavy-duty gumboots and gloves while navigating flooded areas minimized exposure to potential contaminants.

- **Animal Encounters:** The flood brought unexpected visitors like snakes, displaced from their natural habitats. My experience with handling reptiles safely, like rescuing a snake near the hotel periphery, reminded everyone that respecting wildlife and exercising caution are crucial.

- **Structural Integrity:** Before resuming operations, we ensured every area, especially the electrical systems and elevators, were inspected and deemed safe by professionals.

4) Resource Management: Making the Most of Limited Supplies

When resources are scarce, strategic use is critical.

- **Diesel Rationing:** By planning generator usage and prioritizing critical systems, we stretched limited diesel supplies to keep essential operations running.

- **Repurposing Water:** Chlorinated water was used: not just for cleaning but also for sanitation, reducing the need for additional supplies.

- **Food Management:** With fresh supplies inaccessible, rationing food ensured that everyone got enough to sustain themselves until more resources could be procured.

5) Teamwork: The Pillar of Crisis Management

No one person can handle a crisis alone. It was the collective effort of the team, their expertise, and their willingness to go the extra mile that enabled us to recover.

- **Voluntary Contributions:** Yadav, our former store in-charge, exemplified this spirit by volunteering to coordinate labour and logistics for clearing debris. His commitment, even after leaving the organization, was both inspiring and humbling.

- **Delegation:** Trusting the team with tasks like managing submersible pumps, cleaning operations, and guest communications allowed me to focus on critical decision- making.

- **External Support:** Coordinating with external technicians and suppliers for resources like pumps and diesel reinforced the importance of expanding the circle of collaboration in a crisis.

6) Strategic Preparedness – The Importance of Lists in Crisis Management

In any crisis, the foundation of efficient management lies in maintaining accurate and detailed records. Whether it is the team working on the ground or the guests relying on your leadership, understanding **who is present, their skills, and their location** is critical. The experiences during the floods underlined why creating **staff and guest lists** is not just an administrative task but a life-saving strategy.

1) The Significance of a Comprehensive Staff List

A well-maintained staff list provides clarity on the human resources available and their skill sets, enabling optimal task allocation and ensuring safety. Here is why it is essential:

a) Knowing Your Strength

- **Human Resources Inventory**: Each team member brings unique strengths to the table. For example, engineers, housekeeping staff, and valet personnel all contribute differently to managing the crisis.

- **Special Skills**: Identifying specific skills early, like first aid training, mechanical expertise, or logistics knowledge, helps in creating a responsive team that can tackle diverse challenges.

b) Ensuring Safety

- **Headcounts**: Regular headcounts ensure that no staff member is left behind in dangerous areas such as flooded basements or waterlogged areas during flooding or debris removal.

- **Task Monitoring**: A list helps supervisors to keep track of who is assigned where, minimizing risks associated with overexposure to hazardous conditions.

2) Strategic Value of a Guest List

Guests, often seen as individuals requiring care, can sometimes be invaluable contributors in a crisis A detailed guest list ensures their safety and maximizes their potential to assist if needed.

Occupancy Tracking

- **System Backup**: In situations where digital systems are down, having a manual list of room numbers and their occupants is indispensable.
- **Occupied vs. Unoccupied**: Knowing which rooms are vacant helps in efficiently allocating resources and conducting searches during emergencies.

a) Skills Identification

- **Skills Database**: By noting the professions or known skills of guests, you can quickly identify who might be able to help in critical situations. For example:
  - A **doctor** can provide medical assistance.
  - An **electrical engineer** can offer insights into restoring power.
  - An **environmental scientist** can suggest sustainable solutions.
- **Quick Activation**: Guests with relevant expertise can be approached to assist in real- time, providing solutions when outside help is delayed or unavailable.

3) Steps to Maintain Effective Lists in Crisis

Here is a practical guide to building and using these lists effectively:

a) Staff List Maintenance

- Start with a **department-wise breakdown** (e.g., housekeeping, engineering, F&B).
- Note everyone's **specific skill set** beyond their immediate job role (e.g., first aid certification, crisis training, or multilingual capabilities).
- Ensure regular **updates** during the crisis by conducting headcounts every few hours, especially during shifts or task rotations.

b) Guest List Strategy

- Record **room numbers** with the names of all occupants, including dependents.
- Identify **guests with specialized skills** by asking subtle but direct questions during check-ins or interactions.
- Maintain a clear log of **who is present in the property and who has been evacuated** to avoid any confusion during rescue efforts.

c) Coordination and Communication

- Assign a **dedicated team member** to update and manage these lists at regular intervals.
- Use **physical backups** such as whiteboards or printed charts to ensure accessibility even if electronic devices fail.

4) Practical Applications Observed During the Floods

The importance of these lists was evident during the challenges we faced:

- The **staff list** allowed us to manage teams effectively, ensuring safety in high-risk areas like the basement or lift pits. Headcounts conducted regularly avoided any accidental isolation of team members.

- The **guest list** can help us locate occupants quickly, plan their movements, and identify professionals who could assist in critical areas such as medical emergencies or electrical repairs or the ones who needed assistance being elderly or accompanied with minors.

For instance:

- A doctor among the guests can treat minor injuries sustained during clean-up activities or severe medical emergencies.

- A guest engineer can advise on the best methods for water drainage using pumps or troubleshooting any electrical or mechanical equipment necessary for various functions.

5) Lessons Learned and Key Takeaways

1. **Be Prepared**: Start every day in crisis mode by updating these lists. They are as vital as any tool or resource.

2. **Leverage Skills**: Never underestimate the contributions guests or staff can make outside their usual roles.

3. **Ensure Safety**: Headcounts prevent oversights and ensure accountability, especially in high-risk zones.

4. **Stay Organized**: A crisis amplifies confusion; clear, accessible records reduce this significantly.

By maintaining accurate staff and guest lists, you are not only planning for efficient operations but also creating a framework of safety and preparedness. In moments of uncertainty, these simple strategies become the backbone of survival and recovery.

6) Dos and Don'ts: Lessons in Crisis Management
   Do's

- **Plan:** Always have contingency plans for emergencies. In our case, identifying priorities, power, water, and elevators saved valuable time.

- **Communicate Effectively:** Clear instructions and regular updates keep everyone aligned and reduce confusion.

- **Adapt Quickly:** Flexibility in decision-making, such as switching priorities from dewatering the basement to cleaning water tanks, allowed us to address immediate needs efficiently.

- **Document Everything:** Maintaining detailed logs of damage, repairs, and expenses helps in insurance claims and post-crisis audits.

Don'ts

- **Do not Panic:** Decisions made in haste can worsen the situation. Take a moment to assess before acting.

- **Do not Ignore Signs of Exhaustion:** Both physical and mental fatigue can cloud judgment. Ensure proper rest and rotation of responsibilities.

- **Do not Neglect Hygiene:** Floods bring diseases. Regular sanitization of shared spaces and proper disposal of debris are non-negotiable.

- **Do not Isolate Yourself:** Share responsibilities and seek help when needed. Crises are collective challenges, not individual battles.

7) Emotional and Cultural Anchors: Finding Strength in Faith and Celebration

Even amidst the chaos, moments of faith and cultural practices provided emotional stability.

- **Ganesh Chaturthi Celebration:** The arrival of Lord Ganesh's idol marked a turning point. It was not just a religious ritual but a symbol of resilience and renewal. Offering prasad to everyone, I felt a deep sense of gratitude and closure, knowing the crisis had passed.

The Takeaway

This chapter is not just a recounting of strategies but a blueprint for navigating life's tempests. Crises, whether natural or personal, demand a delicate balance of emotions, practicality, and collaboration.

Above all, they remind us of the power of the human spirit. Whether it is finding innovative solutions to seemingly impossible problems, leaning on others for support, or simply holding onto hope, every storm teaches us to rebuild, renew, and thrive.

www.ingramcontent.com/pod-product-compliance
Lightning Source LLC
LaVergne TN
LVHW061610070526
838199LV00078B/7235